2023

LOVING ROBBIE

Alison Whitehead and Drew Stephenson are deeply in love. However, there's an impediment to their happiness . . . Robbie. Alison refuses to marry him unless Drew accepts her teenage son into his life. Secretly, Drew, in an attempt to bond with the boy, takes Robbie on a camping trip, which goes badly wrong. And it's then that Drew begins to find he has a better understanding of Robbie and realises the depths of his love for both Alison and her son.

Books by Kathy George
in the Linford Romance Library:

THE HEART GOES ON
THE OTHER MAN
THE HEALING TOUCH

KATHY GEORGE

LOVING ROBBIE

Complete and Unabridged

LINFORD
Leicester

First published in Great Britain in 2008

First Linford Edition
published 2009

British Library CIP Data

George, Kathy.
  Loving Robbie.—Large print ed.—
Linford romance library
  1. Love stories.
  2. Large type books.
  I. Title
  823.9'2—dc22

  ISBN 978–1–84782–642–8

Published by
F. A. Thorpe (Publishing)
Anstey, Leicestershire

Set by Words & Graphics Ltd.
Anstey, Leicestershire
Printed and bound in Great Britain by
T. J. International Ltd., Padstow, Cornwall

This book is printed on acid-free paper

1

'It isn't working, is it?' Alison said to Drew. Drew said nothing. He was standing on Alison's front doormat with his feet planted wide apart, his deep blue eyes focused not on her, but on some place above her right shoulder.

Alison, in the passage, in the soft glow of hall light, was biting on her lip. She was wearing Drew's thick cable jumper — the white one he'd bought in Edinburgh which was too small for him — over faded blue jeans, and her shiny dark hair was caught up behind her head with something resembling a black chopstick.

She looked, Drew thought, particularly vulnerable, as if the slightest breath of air would blow her over.

He stuffed his hands into his pockets.

'Is it because you're not trying?' Alison said carefully, folding her arms.

Drew inhaled sharply.

'Me? Not trying?'

He heard anger rising in his voice and made an effort to soften his tone.

'Come on, Ali,' he said. 'Give me some credit. I've done all the right things. I've taken him to the movies, bought him popcorn and I've made all the conversation. He never says a word apart from the occasional grunt, he just sits there.' Stuffing his face, Drew thought, but knew better than to say it.

'Keep your voice down,' Alison murmured.

'Sorry.' Drew looked briefly at his feet.

'But really, Ali, he doesn't even offer an opinion on the movie afterwards,' Drew went on, speaking softly. 'He won't say whether he enjoys himself.'

'Does he say thank you?'

'Yes,' Drew admitted.

'Robbie's just a boy,' Alison said. 'You forget — '

'Robbie's fifteen,' Drew interrupted. 'He's almost a man.'

'He's still a boy.'

Drew paused.

'All right, he's still a boy. And, yes, I know teenage boys don't make good communicators.'

He took his hands out of his pockets. 'Look, it's late. I should go.'

Rapidly unfolding her white-cabled arms Alison moved toward him.

'No, don't go when we're like this. Don't go when we're not happy . . . '

Drew said, exasperatedly, 'I don't know what else to do, to say . . . '

She put an overlong sleeve up to his cheeks and he caught it and kissed her protruding fingertips.

'Just say you love me.'

Drew sighed. 'You know I love you.'

'I love you, too,' she said quietly.

'I am going to marry you,' Drew said firmly, pulling her slight body against his. 'I am not going to let this boy stand in my way.'

'This boy?'

Alison recoiled.

'Drew! Robbie's not standing in your

way . . . he's . . . he's standing next to me — not between us. Don't you see? He belongs to me. We belong to each other.' She paused.

'You can't have me without him,' she said finally, tears glistening in her eyes.

Drew, who saw the tears, touched a finger to her lips. Then he turned away from her and strode wordlessly down the garden path.

Inside the house in the study, Alison found her son slouched in front of the computer talking to somebody via the keyboard. She retrieved the black hooded jacket that he had dropped on the floor.

'Time for bed,' she said, picking at a loose thread.

'Just another half-hour.'

'No. You have school tomorrow.'

'I don't.'

'You do. It's Monday tomorrow,' she told him, folding and refolding the jacket.

'Robbie?' She paused. 'How was the movie?'

'Pretty good.'

'Did Drew enjoy it?'

'Yep.'

'Did he say so?'

'I don't know. I don't remember.'

'You don't remember?'

Robbie turned away from the computer screen and looked at Alison from under the thatch of brown hair that covered his forehead and fell into his eyes.

Alison knew that look. It was obstinate and stand-offish. It also regularly appeared when she talked about Drew.

'Yes. I don't remember,' he said stonily. 'Drew's not my father. He never will be. I don't need a father. I'm old enough to look after myself.'

He paused, but Alison didn't say anything. She didn't move away, either.

'Are you finished?' Robbie asked. He turned back to the computer and folded his arms. 'Are we done?'

'Don't be cheeky,' Alison said.

In response Robbie hit the keyboard

with quick, jerky fingers.

'You need a haircut,' Alison told him.

'I do not.'

She put the jacket under her arm, caught his fringe in her fingers and said, 'Look, it's so long I can make a ponytail, and we can put a ribbon in it.'

'Mum,' Robbie said warningly, but he was smiling.

Alison let her hands trail over his thin and bony shoulders as she moved toward the doorway.

'Half-an-hour,' she reminded him as she flicked off the light and left him sitting in the fluorescent glow of the computer screen.

In the bathroom she changed into her pyjamas, brushed her teeth and took off her make-up.

In the bedroom she turned off her electric blanket and slid quietly and neatly under the bedcovers.

She was slightly built and small-boned and she lay in the bed as if she wasn't there, straight and very still, scarcely making a dent under the covers. But her large eyes were open wide, quiet and still like dark pools of water.

In the city of Melbourne, Drew, negotiating a sharp and tight turn into a narrow and dark lane, was only just arriving at the corrugated roller door of his garage. He lived in the inner city, in a thin, tall building which estate agents referred to as 'a loft'.

For Drew, who was sufficiently wealthy not to care either way about real estate, it was a place to stay. More importantly, a place from where he could walk to work, a place that had no garden, save for the three pot plants Alison had grouped together on the rooftop, and therefore no lawns to be mowed and no claim on his time.

But that was all going to change because when they married, Drew was going to live with Alison in Brighton. With Alison and Robbie. In the suburbs. In a cottagey house that had once belonged to her parents when her father had still been alive, with grass that would have to be mowed.

Alison could not be budged from the little white house in Brighton. She said that Robbie needed security and routine, and she could not be budged from that viewpoint either.

Alison wanted Drew to sell the loft when they married. She'd told him that when he worked late back at the office the temptation not to come home to Brighton and to sleep at the loft, would be strong.

If he just once gave in and stayed at the loft, he would be tempted again and again. And she didn't want that; she wanted Drew to come home to her. She wanted the temptation of the loft out of his life.

She knew that what he was doing — marrying someone with baggage, marrying her — was out of character for him, and she knew that having been a bachelor for twenty-something years, Drew was going to have to adapt, not only to her, but to Robbie.

Men like Drew didn't take to change

easily. If the going got tough, it was fairly obvious to Drew that she didn't want him to have a place he could run to.

And yes, Alison knew that Drew had been running from women all his life. She knew a great deal about him. Too much, in fact. Drew suspected she knew that he was more in love with her than she was with him, but that's what came of wanting to marry your personal assistant.

Drew closed the garage door with the remote and trudged up the inner stairs to the first floor and the kitchen. He was tired, but he didn't feel like sleep. He took a beer out of the fridge, flicked its lid and took it and himself up the four flights of stairs to the roof. It was cold out on the roof, the wind blowing straight off Port Philip Bay, but it was where he liked to come and think. He sat down on the concrete, turned up his collar and eased his back against the parapet.

How had he, Drew Stephenson,

practical and analytical, successful —
Managing Director of an international
shipping company — come to do
something as irresponsible as falling in
love with Alison Whitehead, his personal assistant? He still didn't know.

He only knew that one morning,
approximately six months ago now,
Alison had arrived uncharacteristically
late for work. She had stumbled into his
office, presumably to apologise for
being* late, but had stood silently in
front of his desk while the tears
streamed down her face.

'What?' he said. 'What's happened?'
Aghast, he abruptly put down the mug
of coffee he'd had to make himself.

But she couldn't talk. She'd tried to
but she broke out in sobs, and put a fist
up to her mouth. Above her whitened
knuckles, her eyes were stricken. She
looked so frail and slight standing there
in her camel-coloured coat, with her
dark hair all awry and tangled around
her pale face.

He eased her into a chair, closed his

office door discreetly, poured her a drink of water, and fished out a handkerchief.

'Robbie's gone,' she blurted out after a minute.

Robbie? Who was Robbie? Drew tried unsuccessfully to recall what he knew of his personal assistant's personal life. He thought, dimly, that there was a child, a child she'd had when she'd been very young. But Alison wasn't married, he knew that much.

Therefore Robbie was just as likely to be her boyfriend. Somewhat unkindly, he knew that he didn't want to become involved in his assistant's love life.

'Where's this Robbie gone?' he asked lightly.

'I don't know . . . his bed hasn't been slept in. But he — he was home when I went to bed last night,' she paused for a cough, 'but this morning — '

'Have you tried calling him?'

'He's not answering his phone . . . I think . . . I think the battery may be dead.'

11

She twisted and twined Drew's now damp and creased handkerchief in her hands as she spoke. Drew knelt at her side and stilled her hands with one of his large ones.

Alison looked at him. Two bright spots of colour glowed on her ashen cheeks. Her eyes were dark like her hair. Stormy. Almost black.

'Yes?' Alison said. She had an uncanny habit of pre-empting when he was about to speak.

'Where would Robbie normally be at this time?'

'At school.'

Drew breathed out. Ah, he thought, so Robbie was most likely to be her son then.

'Well, let's try the school,' he said, rising from her side. 'Do you know the number?'

'Yes. Of course,' Alison said, quietly reaching for her shoulderbag. 'Why didn't I think of that?'

They found Robbie at school where he should be. They found, after explaining the situation to the headmaster, that Robbie was very cross with his mother over something she'd vetoed and that he'd wanted to punish her. He had, in fact, slept in his bed, succeeded in making it look like he hadn't, and escaped the house before she was awake.

Drew found, standing protectively next to Alison as she spoke to the boy on the phone, that the crown of her head only reached the bottom of his chin. He found — quite to his astonishment — that he wanted to put his arm around her to guard her against boys like Robbie. He wanted to touch her again. But mostly, he wanted to look into her eyes.

Over the following weeks the feeling of wanting to touch her and look at her — even when her hair was smoothly tucked away and her eyes were calm — didn't go away.

Drew fought it, but like Murphy's Law it grew in adverse proportion. It grew into an acute awareness of her presence, a pain he could physically feel. It sent out tendrils that expanded into wanting to cherish her and delight her, wanting to make her laugh, wanting to . . . wanting to marry her.

Marry her? Yes, marry her.

Drew couldn't remember when he'd been so emotionally worked-up over a woman. And it was all the more excruciating because Alison seemed to have no inkling of what she was doing to him.

Drew fought his feelings for Alison because he knew it was uncharacteristic of him to fall for someone like Alison. Drew had dated plenty of other women, but they were usually professional women, certainly not women with children or, in Alison's case, a child. They were women with careers — lawyers or doctors — although once he'd had a frivolous and disastrous relationship with a ballerina.

But it was now alarmingly clear that the sort of woman he needed was one without a career. He knew what it was about Alison that attracted him, what it was about her that made his heart lurch as no other woman had ever succeeded in doing, although the ballerina had come close.

It was Alison's simplicity, her sincerity, her naturalness. It was the fact that she was totally unaware of her beauty, that she had no aspirations, and no mean ambitious streaks. She was, in short, a breath of fresh air.

And she'd had no idea of the turmoil he'd been in.

Up on the roof of his loft, Drew sipped at his beer, remembering with humility his first pathetic efforts to ask her out, not only the first time but a second and a third because she'd said no the first time. She'd said no the second time, too, adamantly.

Alison was aware that anything Drew started would cause waves within the company. She was perceptive, Alison was, forcing Drew to be underhand because the third time he'd asked her out and she'd said no again, somewhat angrily he thought, he'd simply leaned down and kissed her.

That kiss had solved a great deal. It had made it frighteningly clear that he was deeper in love with her than he'd thought. On the positive side, it was clear that Alison returned his love.

When the staff discovered he was dating Alison he'd endured the light-hearted teasing, as he'd endured his father's knowing comments — which he recalled with fondness since his father had known all along what kind of woman Drew needed.

He'd overcome all these hurdles, the most major of which was convincing Alison to marry him and to understand that now he'd found love — the real thing — he wasn't going to give it up, couldn't in fact, only to come up against Robbie.

Robbie. Why was it so hard to form a relationship with a fifteen-year-old boy? A fifteen-year-old who looked under-nourished but wasn't, had big feet and a shock of dark brown hair. Who, Drew suspected, probably smoked behind his mother's back and had a not-so-secret desire to drive Drew's BMW. How could such an insubstantial boy present such an out-of-all-proportion obstacle?

To come this far and be thwarted by a boy was . . . was, well, ludicrous. Laughable.

Drew downed the last of the beer and yawned and stretched, ready for sleep now. But the question of Robbie remained. What to do? How to do it? Alison was adamant that there'd be no marriage without some sort of bond forming between him and Robbie. She was terribly protective of him.

Drew knew why. Robbie had been her rock, the one steadfast male she could rely on all these years as she'd battled through single parenthood and men who'd made commitments and then baulked at the last moment.

Robbie. What, really, did Drew know of boys, apart from the fact that he had once been a boy himself?

Nothing. A big zilch.

He thought of the men he knew who had sons. There was his prospective brother-in-law who had three. He should know about boys, but Drew wasn't convinced he did.

Gregory Whitehead, Alison's brother, was a journalist with the local newspaper, covering the Sports Section, mostly cricket. Intermittently, he insisted that he was trying to get a transfer so that he needn't travel quite so much, but Drew suspected that he was doing nothing of the kind, that Greg actually relished the opportunity to escape his children.

Gregory's boys were, in Drew's personal and very private opinion, nothing more than little devils. None of them were teenagers either, which, Drew concluded, ruled out Gregory's help.

Drew at least knew that teenagers were an entirely different species to children. Of course, when Drew had children, they would be nothing like Gregory's. They would be nothing like Robbie when they were teenagers, either, which brought Drew sharply back to that 'nothing' word.

If you knew nothing on a subject you read up on it, or you visited experts, people who did know, professionals who'd spent years at universities turning their subject inside out and back to front.

There it was, the answer! He would find one of these experts, a psychologist who specialised in adolescents, who knew boys, one who could tell him all the right moves, the right jargon. He would not let this . . . this boy get the better of him.

Drew wanted to marry Alison and he wanted the marriage to work. And, deep down in his heart of hearts, he wanted to experience fatherhood. He wanted a child with Alison.

Sitting against the parapet holding the empty beer bottle in one hand and feeling the chill of the night seep into his bones, Drew realised, quite startlingly, that unless he did something pronto he may never have children, that his dream of a child with Alison might be just that: a dream.

He looked out across the darkness. Between the great hulks of shadowy towering buildings he could just see an elusive sliver of shimmering, shining moonlit sea. To Drew it seemed to be a sign, a sign that just beyond the blackness, the unknown, was happiness.

But would he get there?

2

On Monday morning when Drew came out of his office to greet Alison, she could feel something in the air. It wasn't something she could describe in words, but it was there all the same.

He'd been on the telephone when she'd arrived and she hadn't gone into his office, either to mouth hello or to silently wave with small fingers as she usually did. She'd simply hung up her jacket and pulled out her chair and picked up where she'd left off on Friday.

She smiled at Drew now, but she did not rise or offer her cheek for a kiss. He, in turn, made no move toward her. He stood on the other side of her desk, fiddled with his cuffs and looked at her.

He looked, Alison thought, uncomfortable and untouchable. He was wearing his charcoal suit trousers with a stiff white shirt and striped tie of blue and deep red. He was also wearing the suit jacket as if he was about to go out.

'I have clients,' he said abruptly. 'In the boardroom.'

'You have clients?'

He nodded, distractedly she thought, and continued to fiddle with his cuffs.

Immediately she leaned forward and steadied her hand on her desk calendar. It was a page-a-day calendar which quoted a phrase to inspire productivity, but generally only made Alison feel whimsical and in the mood for a picnic. She saw at a glance that today's quote was 'Never put off until tomorrow what you can do today' and wondered if that was a message for her.

She also saw that the morning of Monday, the twenty-eighty day of April, was empty on her calendar. Blank. Confused, she glanced up at Drew.

'It was arranged late on Friday,' he said. 'Don't you remember? You took the call yourself.'

'I did?'

She had no recollection of taking any call. She lowered her eyes, picked up her pen and put it down again.

'I'm sorry, I don't know why I haven't written it in.'

'It doesn't matter,' he said quietly.

'Oh, but it does. What if you had forgotten?'

'But I didn't forget.'

Drew paused, and then he moved to the door.

'I'll be about an hour, I expect.'

Alison looked up then, but he didn't go. He stood at the door, his hands stilled at his sides, and he stared at her.

After a minute, a minute in which she felt she couldn't breathe and that to tear her eyes away from his would be a confirmation of something she hadn't yet put a name to, he turned on his heel and left.

She knew, of course, what the matter was.

Robbie.

Robbie was the matter. Robbie stood between them like a vast, impenetrable wall of glass. And now Robbie was affecting her work. What was happening, or rather what was not happening between Drew and Robbie, was affecting her work.

Normally, when Alison was cool toward Drew, as she'd been a few times in the last month, Drew tried all the harder. He winked at her when nobody was around and made her blush, he gave her secret smiles in the lift, and he left single red roses lying on her desk. But not today.

Drew returned from his meeting and, with barely a look in her direction, shut himself up in his office. At lunchtime he opened the door that adjoined their offices, stared at her for a minute, mumbled something about going out, and disappeared, neither telling her where he was going or when he would return.

After a minute Alison got up and stood at the large plate-glass window that looked out over Melbourne Docklands, staring into the distance. She wondered if grave doubts were contagious. She'd had them all last week and over the weekend, and now Drew seemed to have them, too.

Drew, she knew, was having trouble accepting Robbie, as other men had, and she could see that mentally he couldn't get around putting her and Robbie together. It was as if he'd taken a snapshot of her and Robbie, torn it in half, put Robbie on one side, her on the other, and inserted himself in the middle.

The issue he could not come to grips with — and this was the crux of the matter — was that Robbie was more important to her than he was.

Alison knew a time would come, not really very far off, when Robbie would go out into the world and make a life for himself. But, in the meantime, she was all Robbie had.

That wasn't quite the truth. He also had a grandmother whom he quite patently adored, and an uncle. But Greg hadn't shown much interest in

Robbie until he'd had children of his own, and the opportunity for Greg to be a father figure to Robbie had never arisen.

Alison had always been both mother and father to Robbie. He had, in fact, no idea who his father was — she had fiercely guarded that secret for years — and Robbie needed to see that she had no intention of deserting him for Drew, that he could remain — until such time as he chose not to — at the core of her life.

Turning abruptly from the window, she reached for her phone and dialled a number.

It was answered somewhat triumphantly on the first ring by a childish voice which no sooner said hello, proceeded to vehemently insist to some other party that there was absolutely no way the receiver was going to be given up just yet.

'Hello?' Alison said tentatively.

'Stevie,' the voice said nasally, 'Stevie speaking.'

'Oh, hullo Stevie,' Alison said. 'This is your Auntie All. What are you up to?' Steven was three and the youngest of Alison's nephews.

'Nothing,' Stevie said, breathing heavily into the phone as if he might possibly have one finger up his nose.

'Is your mummy there?'

'No,' Stevie said firmly.

'Are you sure?'

'She's listening to Liam read,' Stevie said. 'She can't come to the phone.' Then, all in a rush, using quite another voice, an almost hysterical voice, he said,

'And she won't let me go with Liam to soccer because she says I'm too little . . . and I'm not, I'm not little!'

A squeal of protest followed this statement as the phone was wrestled from his hand.

'Hullo?' Alison's sister-in-law said tightly.

'Liz!'

'Ow!' Liz said, grumbling gently. 'The little so-and-so's just kicked me.'

'Are you OK?'

'I will be,' Liz said, 'but he won't be when I get hold of him.' She paused. 'How're things?'

'Good,' Alison said decisively, wondering if Liz could detect the lie in her voice. 'What are you doing on the weekend? We haven't seen you for ages. Is Greg home?'

'Yes, Greg's home,' Liz said, sounding dispirited, certainly not pleased by her husband being home.

'What's wrong?' Ali asked.

'Oh, he's got to go again. He's just got back, hyped the kids up, and now he's got to go to England on a cricket tour. It'll take me a week to settle them again. Honestly, he might as well not have come home.'

'Oh, Liz,' Alison said, grimacing in sympathy. She paused. 'Well, what would you like to do? Would you like to come over for roast dinner on Sunday?'

'Sounds good,' Liz said, 'but you come here.'

'But we always go to you — '

'It's easier for me, Ali. Our house is bigger and there's nothing left to wreck that isn't already wrecked. But you have to bring Robbie, that's the condition. Do you think he could put up with that? You know how much the boys love him.'

The opposite did not hold true. Robbie was quite over his cousins. At first they had been interesting, then amusing, now they were just a pain. He'd told his mother that singly he enjoyed them, but like the flavours of Neapolitan ice-cream they were to be avoided all at once.

★   ★   ★

Drew did not return to the office until well after two-thirty.

Alison thought, looking at him as he breezed through the door, that the worried expression he'd worn before had dissipated, that he seemed decisive and happy about something. She told herself that whoever he'd been to lunch with — because someone must be responsible for the change of demeanour and the faint smile he now wore on his face — it was none of her business. And then.

'Where've you been?' she said sharply.

Drew halted, and turned to look at her as if he was seeing her for the first time.

'Why?'

'Because you're late for the Heads of Department meeting. They're waiting for you in the conference room.'

Drew hated being late for anything. Alison waited for his features to stiffen, for an expression of annoyance to cross his face, or even the utterance of a mild expletive.

'Oh,' he said, still wearing that faint smile. 'Have you — '

'Yes,' she said, 'the papers are on your desk, on your blotter. The agenda is right at the top.'

'Thank you,' he said. The smile broadened. Its warmth reached his dark blue eyes, intensified his gaze, made her feel that no-one else in the world mattered more to him than she did, and her heart missed a beat and went into overdrive the next.

★ ★ ★

It was after five when Drew pushed the door of the conference room closed behind him. He walked quickly, breaking into a trot as soon as he was around the corner. Flinging open the door to the internal stairs, he plunged down them two at a time, pushed through the exit door to the level below, and then steadied himself to a sedate walk down the passage to Alison's office.

But she was gone. Coat, umbrella, both missing, her desk as neat and tidy as his father's suburban back garden. He felt crushed. But what did he expect? It was after five.

He didn't know why he'd wanted to see her so badly. There was nothing he could tell her. Not yet.

He wandered into his office and put

down the papers from the meeting. Several small yellow notes lay on his blotter, messages from Alison. Pouncing on them, he flicked through them, but they were all boring except for the last one which was simply worrying.

Lunch. Sunday, it read. *At Greg and Liz's. Can you come?* Underneath that, Alison had drawn a little heart and signed her name. She had a script which was almost schoolgirlish, and a tendency to dot her i's with small circles and sometimes draw little flowers and hearts on her notes.

Drew peered at the sketch. The heart looked decidedly sloppy, he thought, as if it had been drawn with no real feeling.

He read the note a second time, but the words didn't change. They were still a worry. They were a worry because he couldn't go to Greg and Liz's for lunch on Sunday. And he would have to invent a plausible excuse, telling a lie not only to Ali but to Greg and Liz as well. Crumpling the note up into a ball, he aimed it at the wastepaper basket, threw it, and missed.

★ ★ ★

'I don't want to tell Alison,' Drew said.

'Why ever not?' his father asked.

'She'll spend the weekend worrying, fuss too much, ring us up all the time. And she'll expect too much. She'll expect us to come back best mates. Whereas . . . whereas I don't even know if it's going to work,' Drew said moodily.

His father refolded his paper napkin and placed it alongside his empty plate.

'I know why you don't want to tell her,' he said quietly.

Drew put down his knife and fork. 'You think you know.'

His father said nothing.

Drew moved his beer glass through a ring of condensation on the wooden table.

'All right,' he said. 'Tell me.'

Harry sipped at his beer.

He said, 'You don't want to tell Ali because you want her to think you don't know it all. It's my bet you won't even tell her you went to see somebody, a professional, a psycho-whatsit, to get advice. You'd like to pass off that this camping trip, this bonding session you want to do with Robbie, is all your own idea.'

His father paused and cleared his throat noisily, which was a sign to Drew that he was going to say something Drew probably didn't want to hear.

'Furthermore, I don't believe you have any real intention of bonding with the boy.'

'I don't?' Drew said faintly. 'Well, thank you.'

'If you did you would tell Ali what you were doing. She's his mother, she needs to know.'

'She doesn't,' Drew said stoutly. 'She knows too much already.'

'That's your opinion,' Harry said. He paused. 'I assume you told me all this because you wanted an opinion?'

'Well . . . yes,' Drew said uneasily.

Harry said nothing. He raised his glass and in one smooth swallow emptied it. Then he hauled himself up from his chair, somewhat heavily Drew thought, and went to the bar counter, clutching the two empty glasses.

The heaviness with which his father had vacated his seat reminded Drew that Harry was sixty-five. Sixty-five and, although he never mentioned it, longing for a grandchild. Oh yes, Drew had seen the way his father looked at passing babies, at toddlers.

There'd been one in the pub earlier, sitting in a high chair. His father had wasted little time in making eye-contact, then pulling a face, encouraging the kid to laugh.

Drew had dinner with his father on every last Monday of every month. Drew's mother had passed away in England on the last Monday of a February eight years ago, and after Drew had brought his father out to Australia, they had fallen into the habit of getting together on the last Monday of every month in her memory.

They had been a close family. In the summer, on their get-togethers, his father often brought fish and chips and they went down to the beach. Sometimes Drew cooked, which he was good at, but more often than not, and especially in winter, they went to a bayside pub where there was a roaring fire. This was where they were tonight.

Of course, Drew had dinner with his father at other times too, or lunch, or they went to the football together. Once they'd taken Robbie to the football. Robbie had seated himself next to Harry, and in between mouthfuls of pie and sauce had chatted amiably and voluntarily to Harry, but every time Drew tried to get in a sentence or two, Robbie had clammed up.

His father had told him he was trying too hard.

Now, returning with two more beers, Harry pushed one across to Drew.

'How do you think you are going to

accomplish this . . . trip, this camping, trekking thing without Ali knowing?'

'I'm going to ask Zelma for help.'

'Zelma?' Harry raised his eyebrows.

Harry had more than once expressed the opinion to Drew that Zelma's name suited her to the letter. She was zany and zealous. She was known to dress in brazen colours like a zebra, and he suggested her home could probably be classified as a zoo of sorts.

She had goldfish, two dogs and three cats. She hung honey and seed contraptions from trees outside her window, over which lorikeets and rosellas fought and bickered and made an awful din. Considering she was Alison's mother, Harry had told Drew that she was not like Alison at all.

'And how precisely is Zelma going to be of help?'

'I don't know yet,' Drew said. 'I'm working on it.'

'You got your phone?' Harry asked, glancing at his watch as if Drew didn't have much time.

37

Drew nodded, swallowing beer.

'Call her,' Harry said. 'Tell her we're coming round and we'll be there in half-an-hour.'

'What? Go around there now?'

'Why not? You know she keeps odd hours.'

'But how's she going to help if *I* don't yet know how she's going to help.'

'She's the boy's grandmother,' Harry said patiently. 'She'll think of something.'

3

Zelma was in the middle of things. 'Oh, it's you,' she said preoccupiedly when she eventually appeared to answer the door, as if she'd already forgotten Drew and Harry were coming, although ten minutes had scarcely elapsed since she'd spoken to Drew.

Evidence of her being in the middle of things was on her hands, some sort of cement-coloured matter, which Drew thought might be plaster. He was now embarrassed to be disturbing her, but there'd been no reference to any activity when he'd called. However, it did explain why the phone had rung for a considerable time before she'd answered it.

When the noise of the two barking dogs subsided, she led them down the wooden-floor passage, not into the living-room which was on the right, but down toward the rear of the house into the kitchen. They made a little procession. Drew traipsing along behind Zelma, sidestepping shaggy golden-haired retrievers, following the back of her torn and overlarge shirt, which probably had once belonged to Alison's father he thought, and Harry bringing up the rear.

The kitchen was in its usual shambles of clutter and unwashed dishes and glasses, but this time the table was not covered in today's newspaper opened at the crossword page, but simply with sheets of newspaper. On top of that stood a wet clay sculpture that looked remarkably like a magpie alighting on a rock.

Drew, studying the sculpture, said, 'This is very good.'

'It's getting there,' Zelma said, 'But it takes time.'

She leaned over, made a small indentation with her thumb in the magpie's tail, and stood back to survey the effect with narrowed eyes.

Harry pulled out a kitchen chair and

sat down near a large platter of antipasto which was half hidden under a tea-towel.

Zelma pushed the platter closer. 'My supper,' she said. 'Have a dolmades.'

Harry gingerly picked up a stuffed vine leaf and held it carefully between two fingers as if it might bite.

Zelma, in contrast, scooped up a slice of marinated dried tomato and a chunk of Brie with a cracker and put all three in her mouth at once, dribbling juice down her chin.

Nobody said anything. Drew noticed that the oven was on but empty, its door flung open wide, filling the kitchen with necessary warmth. The dogs lay in front of it as it was a blazing fire, taking up what little floor space there was.

Only Zelma would think of putting on the oven to warm up the kitchen. She was a very practical woman. Come to think of it so was Alison.

His father wasn't completely right then, there were some similarities between mother and daughter. Not to mention the fact that they both had big, dark eyes.

Alison.

Robbie.

He sighed.

This was why they were here, wasn't it?

'I've come about Robbie,' he said uncomfortably, looking at Harry, who was still holding the uneaten stuffed vine leaf.

Zelma glanced sternly at Drew from under dark and well-shaped eyebrows.

'Finally,' she said, wiping juice from the corner of her mouth with one finger and leaving a white plastery mark.

Drew wasn't sure whether she was rebuking him for taking so long to get to the point, or whether it was because he'd taken forever to do something about Robbie.

He glanced at his father again for support, but Harry had picked open one end of the vine leaf and was studying its contents.

Drew wished he was close enough to

kick him under the table.

'Well?' said Zelma.

'I want to take Robbie away for the weekend.'

'Lovely,' said Zelma, concentrating on smoothing a wet hand over one over the magpie's legs.

'And?' she said a minute later into the silence.

'He wants to do it without Alison knowing,' Harry told her, in a tone of voice that indicated he thought Drew was making a mistake and that he hoped Zelma would back him up.

But Zelma merely said, 'Of course.'

She stopped fiddling with the magpie, opened the fridge door and peered inside. Withdrawing an uncorked bottle of white wine, she poured herself and Drew two generous glasses and held out the bottle to Harry questioningly.

But Harry declined. The dolmades had disappeared and he was smearing his fingers on the newspapered table.

Drew suspected that the dog now looking lovingly up at Harry and licking

its lips was involved in its disappear-
ance.

'The problem is,' Drew said, 'how to
keep it away from Alison.'

'Of course,' said Zelma again.

She took a gulp of wine, dragged a
chair over to the table, and sat down.
She looked at Drew.

'The answer is simple. Tell her you
have to go away for the weekend. On
business. Ali can't question that. Business is business. And Robbie must
come here.'

'Yes,' Drew said slowly, 'But why?
Why will he come to you? We need to
have a good reason, something that Ali
will agree to . . . and believe.'

Zelma put down her wine glass,
pulled out a hair clip and attempted to
restore order in the mess that was piled
on top of her head. Drew knew she was
thinking.

She was an attractive woman for her
age. In the early days Drew had had
thoughts of pairing her off with his
father, but that was before he knew her

properly. He now believed they were far too dissimilar to even be attracted to one another, let alone live companionably together.

'I've got it,' Zelma said slowly 'I'll tell Ali I want to do a sculpture of Robbie and that's why I need him for the weekend. I've always wanted to. Just his head you understand.'

'But won't Ali want to see it?'

'Ali knows not to disturb me when I'm working.'

'But you'll really have to do a sculpture of Robbie without him to complete the deception. You know that, don't you?' Harry said.

'Yes, I know that,' Zelma said breezily.

'And can you?' Drew asked, presumptuously he knew, but he had to be certain that it was all going to work.

Zelma made a snort of derision and clapped her hands together sharply. The dogs half-rose at the sudden noise and began to bark.

'Oh, be quiet!' she said goodnaturedly. She finished the last of her wine in one gulp and leaned across the table.

'Have another vine leaf, Harry,' she said, pushing the antipasto platter in his direction. 'They're rather good, aren't they?'

One problem was now safely sorted, but there still remained at least one other. How to tell Robbie about the camping trip without Alison's knowledge?

Or rather, how to ask Robbie. You didn't tell a teenager anything these days, the psychologist had told Drew. You negotiated or you made suggestions or requests and hoped that you'd be taken up on them.

The thing was that it was difficult to get Robbie on his own. Drew tried calling his school, but the receptionist said that messages were only passed on to students in an emergency, and as this clearly wasn't an emergency and Drew clearly wasn't even related to Robbie, she was sorry but it clearly didn't qualify.

Next Drew tried calling the house in the afternoons, but Robbie was strangely never there. He got the answer machine and a recording of Alison's sweet voice time and time again. He wondered if Ali knew that Robbie didn't go home straight after school.

At lunchtime he slipped out of the office, caught a taxi to Robbie's school and hung around the perimeter, hoping to catch a glimpse of him. But as any parent knows it is extremely hard to single out one's own child amongst a horde of others similarly dressed.

It didn't take long for someone to single out Drew, however. A patrolling teacher. She began to advance upon him in a business-like manner, her cellphone at the ready.

'Excuse me,' he called out.

'Yes,' she said sharply coming up to the fence.

'I'm looking for Robbie Whitehead,' Drew told her. 'You wouldn't know — '

'And who are you?' she said sharply again.

'Drew Stephenson.' He put his hand over the fence to shake hers, but the teacher didn't move from where she stood.

She said, 'What is your relationship to Robbie Whitehead?'

'I'm going to be his step-dad,' Drew told her. The word sounded odd to his ears.

He rested his hands on the fence. 'I need to talk to him because I'm taking him away for the weekend so that we can, um,' he made a gesture in the air, 'bond,' he said.

The teacher's expression softened. She lowered her arms, which had been tensed at her sides as if for a fight.

'Can I see some identification?' she said.

Drew took out his wallet and showed her his driver's licence, then he passed across one of his business cards.

'Wait here,' she said and turned to the handful of overgrown children who had, by now, gathered at her back like goats and were staring at Drew.

'Who's seen Robbie Whitehead,' she said to them.

A hand shot up. 'I have, miss. He's on the oval, playing footie.'

'Go,' she said to the boy, who was taller than she was, 'run. Tell him I want to see him. Here. Now.'

After a minute, she turned to Drew. 'Where are you going for the weekend?'

'Wilson's Prom,' he said, putting away his wallet.

'I hope the weather holds.'

Drew nodded. 'I hope so, too.'

'It can get cold there quite unexpectedly, this time of the year,' she told him.

Drew nodded. In the distance he could see Robbie, coming at a run, the other boy in tow.

'Here he comes,' Drew said unnecessarily.

The teacher took a few steps back. 'You won't mind if I don't go just yet, will you?' she said, smiling apologetically. 'It's just a precaution.'

'Of course not,' Drew said.

Robbie, at the fence now, his face

white, stared at Drew, barely acknowledging the teacher.

'It's nothing,' Drew said quickly, realising that he had frightened the boy and that he ought to have been more circumspect.

'I mean, your mother's fine. She doesn't know I'm here. I, um — '

'Whatdya want, then?' Robbie interrupted, stepping away and putting his hands on his hips to draw air into his heaving chest.

'I'm trying to tell you,' Drew said patiently.

Robbie lowered his eyes.

'I'm going away for the weekend, to Wilson's Prom. Camping. I want to know whether you'd like to come?'

'What?' Robbie said, coming to the fence again. 'Just you and me?'

'Yes,' Drew said levelly. 'Just you and me.'

'All right,' Robbie said. 'When?' He was clutching the fence now, looking at Drew, the thick wad of hair falling over his forehead and into his eyes.

'Saturday morning, early.'

'Can't,' Robbie said. 'I've got football.'

Drew closed his eyes.

'Can't you miss the game, just this once?'

'I suppose,' Robbie said. 'I'll have to ask.'

'Now, the important bit,' Drew said, speaking slowly. 'We are not telling your mother.'

'We're not?'

'No. She'll fuss. Worry. You know what she's like.'

'Yes,' Robbie said simply.

'I need you to tell her that your grandmother has asked you to come over for the weekend. She wants to do a sculpture of you.'

'She does?' Robbie frowned. 'Really?'

'Yes,' Drew said. 'She does. Really, really.'

Robbie gave him a withering look.

Drew took no notice. 'You'll go over there on Friday evening. Take all the warm clothing you have. A jumper, a parka, long pants. I'll pick you up from your grandmother's early on Saturday morning — '

The sound of the school bell pierced the air, putting an end to any further conversation. Walking backwards, Robbie began to move away from the fence. His tie was skew, Drew saw, and his jumper ripped along the sleeve. He also had a smear of mud down one cheek.

He looked, Drew had to admit, like a ragamuffin, a delinquent. Alison would be horrified.

'What about a sleeping bag?' Robbie called out, still looking at Drew. His head was slightly tilted so that he could see Drew from under all the hair.

'Do you have one?'

'Nah,' Robbie said.

'Then I'll bring you one.'

Robbie was still looking at him. Drew hesitated, wondering if there was something he'd forgotten to tell the boy, but he didn't think so. Although, come to think of it, there was something that wouldn't go astray.

'You could have a haircut,' he called out.

'What?' Robbie said, cupping a hand to one ear.

'A haircut,' Drew called out again. 'You need a haircut.'

'Sorry.' Robbie was shouting. 'Can't hear you.'

He held up the fingers of one hand vertically and bounced the palm of the other on top of the fingers, clearly indicating he had to go, and ran off.

Walking back to the waiting taxi, Drew thought it was odd that Robbie had said he couldn't hear him, since he'd been able to hear Robbie perfectly clearly.

★ ★ ★

'Are you sure?' Alison said, standing at Ellen's desk.

'Of course I'm sure,' Ellen almost snapped.

Ellen was the office manager of the shipping company where Drew and Alison worked.

'If there's a conference, I'd know about it. As I don't know about it, it can mean only two things: Drew has got his dates muddled up, or — '

She paused meaningfully but didn't put her thoughts into words. Raising her eyebrows, she went back to her computer screen.

Alison paused, her finger tapping unconsciously on Ellen's wooden desk, and her eyes focusing on nothing.

Would Drew lie to her?

'Thank you, Ellen,' she said. 'Thank you.'

In her own office, she slipped quietly into the seat behind her desk. The interleading door to Drew's office was closed. Drew was with clients, and she could hear muffled voices coming from behind it.

This weekend, he'd told her all in a rush in the minutes before the clients had arrived, he'd be away. There was a conference, a business conference, he said. He didn't know why he hadn't told her before, it must have slipped his mind. He was sorry, he said. Sorry.

It was already Thursday afternoon, one day until the weekend. In Alison's opinion, a bit late to tell her that he was going to be away for the weekend. It had been a relatively peaceful Thursday afternoon up until then, but now Alison wasn't feeling the least bit peaceful.

On her desk, alongside her computer was a yellow notepad. At the top of the notepad it said, *Lunch Sunday Liz and Greg*, followed by *Drew* and a series of question marks.

Alison picked up a pen, leaned forward and scratched out *Drew* and the question marks. She underlined the sentence twice, and the second time she pushed so hard on the pen it ripped the page.

★   ★   ★

Drew glanced at his watch. His clients had gone an hour ago and it was now ten to five. Ten minutes until Alison left to go home. And she would go

55

promptly today. She was up to date with everything.

He'd seen earlier that her desk was clear, that she'd even gone so far as to remove everything and polish the desk — a faint whiff of beeswax hung in the air — which she was wont to do when she was bored. He was surprised he'd been capable of taking in that detail, concentrating as he was on the lie that'd come out of his mouth.

Strange that she'd said nothing about Robbie not being able to go to Liz and Greg's for lunch, either. Strange that Alison had said nothing full stop, almost as if she didn't trust herself to speak. She hadn't looked at him, either.

Drew closed his eyes. He didn't blame her. He'd lied to her. He wouldn't look at himself either if he were her.

If only he didn't have to keep this weekend with Robbie away from her. If only . . .

But, apart from anything else, Drew had no certainty it was going to be a success or even work.

On Monday when he'd seen the psychologist it had all seemed perfectly straightforward and quite within his grasp. And now quite simply . . . now it didn't. And if there was a chance of failure, Drew didn't want Alison — didn't want anybody for that matter — to know about it.

Drew glanced at his watch again. Five to five now. He pushed his chair back, stood up and made his way to the interleading door. He couldn't let her leave tonight without some sort of gesture, some sort of reassurance that although things had been frosty between them all week, he loved her.

What he would say or do, he had no idea. He hoped that when he opened the interleading door, the sight of her would inspire him to do and say the right thing, as the sight of her lovely face so often did.

On the other side of the office wall, Alison glanced at her watch. It was still a few minutes to five, but she was up to date with everything and she couldn't see the point in waiting for the minutes to expire. She wanted to go. She felt uncomfortable.

Drew hadn't really spoken to her since Sunday night, and she had this disquieting feeling that the beginning of the end had been set in motion. What she'd dreaded happening when Drew began to go out with her, was starting to happen. She would have to find a new job now, she couldn't go on working for Drew or the company.

Everybody knew about them being an item, and everybody would know that the relationship was over, would know that Drew had baulked at taking on the responsibility of Robbie.

She picked up her shoulder bag and swung it over one shoulder. Then she draped her overcoat over her arm, and reached decisively for the handle of the interleading door.

But it opened quickly, far too quickly. The handle was, in fact, wrenched out of her hand and she fell forwards into the room. Bumping her nose painfully on the door, she dropped her coat.

'Ow,' she said, clutching her nose, her eyes smarting. 'Ow.'

'Alison! Oh, Ali,' Drew said at the same time. 'I am so sorry. So sorry.'

He ferreted in his pocket for a handkerchief and pushed it gently to her nose.

'Does it hurt badly?' he asked.

But Alison didn't reply, couldn't reply most probably Drew thought.

'It's bleeding,' he said with concern, a second later.

'Ohhh,' Alison said in a wobbly voice. She felt as if her nose had swollen to ten times its normal size.

The pain, at any rate, was beyond comprehension, so severe that she didn't realise, until it was too late, that she was going to faint.

* * *

When she came to, she was propped up against the door, and Drew was on his knees beside her, urgently saying her name over and over again. He sounded distraught.

'It's all right,' she said matter-of-factly. 'I'm here.'

'Thank goodness.'

'Is it broken, do you think?'

'No,' said Drew. 'I don't think so. It's already stopped bleeding if that's any consolation.'

'I was coming to say goodbye,' Alison said, pushing the handkerchief away from her face.

'Yes, I know. I guessed that much.' Drew looked hard at her.

Alison wondered if he knew just how close to really saying goodbye she was.

She tried to rise, but Drew pushed her back down.

'You're not going anywhere for a little while,' he said. 'First I'm going to get some ice and then I'm going to take you home.'

'No,' Alison said, 'I don't want you to.'

'I know you don't want me to,' Drew

told her, 'but going home on the train tonight by yourself is not an option. Not with a nose like Rudolph's. Sorry,' he said.

Alison thought that he didn't sound the least bit sorry. To her ears he sounded distinctly annoyed.

★   ★   ★

She was right. He was annoyed.

In the car on the way home, Drew, knowing it was selfish, could only think of all the things he still had to do on top of now driving Alison home.

He had to go around to his father's, find the three-man tent which must be in the garage since Drew couldn't find it anywhere in his loft, unearth his mess kit, locate the small cooker in case it was too damp to light a fire, check whether he needed to get gas for the cooker, and assemble some food, enough for two lunches, a dinner and a breakfast.

Alison said, abruptly. 'What time will

you get home on Sunday night from — from this conference?'

She was still holding his bloody handkerchief, Drew noticed, curled up into a tight ball inside her fist.

'I'm not sure,' he said vaguely, wondering what sort of walker Robbie was, and how far they would get on the first day. 'I'll have to see what time we finish.'

'Will you,' she said. 'I mean, can you — can you call me when you get back?'

Drew took his eyes off the road and glanced at her, but she was looking at her lap.

'I know it might be late,' she said, 'but can you do that for me? Call me?'

She raised her head, and he saw that she had tears in her eyes.

'Yes,' Drew said. 'I can do that.'

He wondered if his diagnosis was wrong. She was still in pain obviously. Perhaps her nose was broken after all.

He turned his attention back to the road, and as he did so he caught a fleeting glimpse of a camping shop at the side of the Nepean highway. And in that fleeting glimpse he saw, too, that the camping shop was open.

He began to say something, realised that this was not the person he should be sharing the need for an additional sleeping bag with, and made a noise that sounded as if he was being strangled instead.

Coughing and clearing his throat in what he hoped was not a suspicious fashion, he looked at Alison out of the corner of his eye. But she sat quietly, oblivious to him, or so it seemed. Reaching over, he put a hand over one of hers. It was freezing.

'You're cold,' he said in astonishment.

'Yes,' she said.

'Why didn't you say so?' he said, turning on the car's heating.

In answer she withdrew her hand from under his. She turned away, almost deliberately it seemed to look out of her side window.

Drew tapped his fingers on the steering wheel and screwed up his face as if he had an excruciating pain in his back molar.

He should never have admitted to Alison that his relationship with Robbie was a non-event. But in all seriousness he couldn't see how he could have avoided telling her.

His mother had always told him that communication between men and women wasn't good at the best of times, that in a marriage, well, you simply had to work at it even harder.

Wee, small things, she'd told him in her Scottish brogue, could sometimes grow into elephantine misunderstandings if there was no communication.

Admitting to Alison that he had a problem with Robbie had been the right thing to do. His mother would have been pleased. He was communicating. But he just couldn't admit to her that he was taking steps to improve his relationship with Robbie. He wanted it simply to happen, to be a done thing.

But there was something else too, he realised, something he hadn't put into words. He wanted Alison to be aware that he could handle any parenting crisis that came his way, that, most importantly, he could be relied upon to be pro-active in the area of fatherhood.

If she was going to have his child after their marriage, these were very important matters to accomplish early on. It wasn't to be taken for granted that she would want to have more children. What if she didn't? He bit the bottom of his lip. It didn't bear thinking about.

When they reached the little white cottage in Brighton, Alison opened the car door and got out practically before the vehicle was stationary.

'Thank you for the lift,' she said stiffly, standing alongside the open door.

Drew leaned over and gazed up at her. He thought briefly about asking for a goodbye kiss and just as briefly dismissed the idea as inappropriate. He remembered that before Alison had injured herself he'd been on his way to reassure her of his love. To his alarm he realised that he still hadn't done that.

'Ali,' he said urgently.

But putting the handkerchief up to her nose and speaking nasally, Alison said, 'Not now.'

She closed the car door, walked up the path to her front door, unlocked it and let herself in without once looking back at Drew.

4

Harry lifted up the telephone receiver and put it down again. He picked up his little telephone book — brown leather, serviceable — and looked up the number for the second time. This time he said the number out loud as he pressed the corresponding buttons. But before the phone began to ring, he put it down once more.

He stared at the hall table on which the telephone sat. Then, with the sleeve of his jumper pulled across his palm, he smoothed his hand across its polished wooden surface, leaving clear evidence of the path his hand had taken.

Suddenly the telephone rang shrilly, making him jump.

'Hello?' he said tentatively.

'Harry?'

'Yes?'

'What are you doing, Saturday?'

'Nothing,' he said to Zelma. 'Well, nothing that can't wait.'

'Good,' she said. 'I'd like you to come over. I will need some help with this sculpture.'

'You will?' Harry said faintly.

'Yes, I will. Proportions, sizing, that sort of thing. About lunch-time if you don't mind. I'll make some scones.'

She hung up. She didn't say goodbye. And somehow Zelma's not saying goodbye didn't strike Harry as at all odd. It was behaviour Harry might have expected from Zelma.

Nevertheless, Harry took the receiver away from his ear and looked at it. He didn't think that Zelma had ever rung him before. But apart from that, what was really odd he decided, was that she had called him when he had been trying — and trying was the operative word here — to ring her. It was almost as if she had sensed his need to communicate with her.

He left the hall and went into the laundry to get the dust cloth and the furniture polish. After he had removed everything from the hall table, dusted it down and polished it, he went into the back garden where he vigorously raked up autumn leaves.

When that was done, he spread the leaves over the compost heap. Then he felt compelled, in view of the fact that it had turned into a warm and sunny day, to clear the front garden bed of weeds, and to mow all three lawns, front, back and nature strip.

After lunch and a nap, he tackled the bougainvillea down the side of the driveway and cut it back. It was almost he thought, as he extracted a particularly stubborn thorn from his finger, as if he was preparing the house and garden for an event of some magnitude. A change. Like . . . like a sale. A sale? The idea was nonsense. Why would he want to sell up his house and live elsewhere?

When Drew turned up later in the evening to hunt for his camping gear, Harry didn't tell him about being invited to Zelma's on Saturday. Or about his sudden activity in and outside the house. For reasons best known only to himself, it wasn't information he felt inclined to share.

★ ★ ★

In the camping shop the sales assistant, who was dressed in khaki like a safari guide but had dreadlocks unlike any safari guide Drew had ever met, pointed out that there were two types of sleeping bag available.

One was down and very expensive. The other was made of nylon and artificial filler and consequently a great deal cheaper. Drew felt both of them for thickness. They felt similar, but Drew knew enough about sleeping bags to know that denseness and ability to keep the heat in and the cold out, were not the same thing.

Drew's own sleeping bag was like the former, down and expensive. He'd had it for years, and it had never failed to keep him snug and warm.

He told the sales assistant to give him a few minutes to think it over. The possibility of buying himself a new sleeping bag and giving his old one to Robbie had crossed his mind and he needed to think it through. But, he reasoned with himself, you didn't usually sleep in other people's sleeping bags, not unless you'd had them thoroughly dry-cleaned beforehand and even then it wasn't something Drew would ever have done. Why should he make Robbie? Sleeping bags were very personal things, like hairbrushes or toothbrushes.

Drew didn't know why he needed to think about the choice. If he was buying the sleeping bag for himself there was no doubt as to which one he would choose. But he wasn't, was he? He was buying it for Robbie.

So? he asked himself, why was he hesitating? What difference did it make? He reached for the expensive, down sleeping bag and told himself that if he'd been buying the sleeping bag for his own son — his own son — the thought sent shivers down his spine, this was clearly the choice he would have made.

At the cash register, waiting for the assistant with dreadlocks to process his credit card, he realised that he had to start thinking of Robbie in terms of being his son.

The psychologist had told him that he should think about Robbie in terms of being his friend, not his son, but Drew was inclined to think — much as he knew the man had spent years studying up on this — that the psychologist was wrong on this particular point. How could Robbie possibly come to accept Drew as his father if Drew didn't treat him like a son?

* * *

'I'm not going to come,' Alison said to her brother, Greg.

'Come again,' he said.

'Lunch on Sunday,' Alison said patiently. 'At your place . . . Liz invited us . . . but I'm not going to come.'

She waited for the information to sink in.

'Why?' her brother said.

'Well, it'll just be me. It hardly seems worth it. Robbie can't come and neither can Drew,' she said stiffly. 'And we can't invite Mum, either.'

'We can't?'

'No, she's doing a sculpture with Robbie. She doesn't want to be contacted the entire weekend.'

'Oh,' Greg said. 'Right. I'll tell her then, I'll tell Liz.'

Alison paused. 'Is Liz there?' she asked.

'No. She's out doing the shopping.'

'But why is it so quiet? Where are the boys? She hasn't taken them with her, has she?'

'No, of course not. They're out the back, playing on the soccer field.'

'In the dark? You've left them alone on the soccer field in the dark?'

'The phone rang!'

'Since when has a phone ringing in your house made a difference to you, Gregory Whitehead?'

'I'm expecting a call,' Greg said. 'I'm always expecting calls, you know that.'

'Right,' Alison said. 'Then I'd better hang up.'

'Are you all right?' her brother asked. 'You sound a bit, um, a bit — '

'I'm fine,' Alison snapped.

Her brother said nothing.

'Greg?'

'Yes.'

'Tell Liz to call me sometime, OK?'

Alison put down the receiver and automatically reached up to touch her nose, which was something she did when she was close to tears, but she had forgotten her nose was still very sore.

'Ouch,' she said out loud. 'Ouch.'

In the kitchen, on the countertop, she found the tissues and wiped her eyes. The sink, she saw, was full of dirty dishes and unwashed pots from dinner were still standing on the stove. Normally Alison cleaned up as soon as they had eaten, but not tonight.

Tonight everything — not only her nose — seemed out of kilter.

Down the passage, Robbie's bedroom door was shut. She knocked and waited for permission to enter, but it took a long time for Robbie to respond. Alison tilted her head. She could hear something that sounded distinctly like Robbie rummaging in his cupboards.

But when he opened his door, everything appeared as it should. Messy to the usual degree — towel and dirty socks on the floor, school trousers lying exactly where he'd stepped out of them, used tissues alongside but not in the bin — but no different to how the room had looked that morning. Over Robbie's shoulder, Alison saw that his cupboard doors were shut. Unusual, but not unheard of.

'Yup?' Robbie said, the annoying fringe hanging in his eyes. He looked flushed as if he'd been bending over, as if he'd been rummaging in his cupboards.

'What are you doing?' Alison said.

'Nothing,' Robbie said.

Alison waited. He made as if to shut the door, but she caught it lightly against her fingertips.

'You must be doing something,' she said.

'Well actually I was looking for a piece of Lego,' he said in a considered way.

'Lego?' Robbie hadn't, to Alison's knowledge, played with Lego for years.

'Yes, Lego,' Robbie said firmly.

'Do you need a hand?' Alison asked, peering over his shoulder again into his room.

'No,' Robbie said firmly.

Alison paused.

'Have you done your homework?'

'I haven't got any.'

'What? No homework at all?'

'No, Mum. Not today. It does happen that we don't get homework.'

'Then you can help me with the dishes!'

A slight frown crossed Robbie's face.

'In a minute,' he said. 'In a minute when I've found that Lego.'

He tilted his head to one side and examined her.

'Is your nose sore?' he asked.

She nodded, feeling the closeness of the tears again.

'Have you taken something for it? Like a painkiller?'

'A painkiller?' she echoed, stepping back from the door. 'No I haven't,' she said. 'I don't know why . . . why I didn't think of that. Thank you, Robbie,' she said quietly.

'That's OK.'

He looked hard at her as if he'd worked out that something more than her injured nose, his long hair and the dirty dishes was worrying her, but didn't know how to begin to put it into words.

'I'll see you in a minute, then . . . for the dishes?' she said hopefully.

'Yes, Mum,' he told her and closed the door.

★   ★   ★

When Alison got to work on Friday morning, she took off her coat and hung it behind her chair and placed her shoulderbag in the bottom drawer of her desk as she always did. Then she took off her engagement ring, put it into her palm and gazed at it for one last time.

It was a beautiful ring. When Drew gave it to her, he told her that it had been his mother's and that he would understand if she wanted to choose a ring of her own, that what his mother had liked might not necessarily be to Alison's taste.

But she had adored the ring right from the start. It was gold and very plain, and the small diamond was set well back into the thick band. Alison loved it for its simplicity. When it was on her finger there was something very solid and genuine-looking about it. Eternal. It had fitted her perfectly, too, as if it had been meant for her finger and no-one else's.

She distinctly remembered Drew sliding it on to her finger, remembered where she and Drew were when he'd asked her to marry him, what he'd been wearing, what he'd said and how he had said it.

Suddenly, she was angry. How could Drew do this to her? What kind of mean-spirited man was he? To lead her on, to promise her roses and champagne and happy-ever-afters, and now . . . this!

She closed her palm over the ring. She was shaking, not with nerves but with rage. She knocked on Drew's door and when he called out she opened the door and went in.

'Look,' she said, almost belligerently.

And Drew, pen in hand, looked up from the paperwork on his desk, looked up at her and met her eyes with slow deliberation — his own eyes very blue and intense in the early morning light — and everything she had planned to say went out of the window.

Clenching her jaw, she very carefully prised the ring out from under her fingers and, with a trembling hand, placed it on the smooth yellow wood of Drew's desk, in a space between the edge of his white blotter and a pile of correspondence.

The ring wobbled a little before it lay still, wobbled as if nervous about suddenly being left on its own. The light caught its deep golden colour and twinkled around the small white gem in its centre and, for a moment, Alison thought it was simply the most beautiful ring she was ever likely to see.

She raised her teary eyes. Drew, she saw in a blur, had not moved, and although it appeared to her that his mouth had opened, gone slack in fact, he hadn't said anything either, and obviously wasn't going to.

His silence and his lack of action confirmed everything she'd suspected.

Everything being that she was convinced that since Sunday, Drew had decided he was not prepared to take on

Robbie, that he did not have the courage to tell her so.

Alison, blind with tears, turned awkwardly. She stumbled over the Persian rug in front of Drew's desk but managed to get to the door without falling. Closing it behind her, she located her coat and her shoulderbag by feel and, as quickly as she could, left the office.

On the walk to the station she composed herself, and by the time she caught the train back home only her head throbbed. She rested it against the cold glass of the train window, relieved that her tears had gone.

She seemed to be very calm, abnormally calm. In spite of the fact that it was possible she had acted rashly.

Yesterday, she had decided not to do anything rash until Sunday night when Drew returned from the conference and rang her. But this morning, on her way to work, after a sleepless night, she'd realised that she couldn't bear the suspense another minute. She needed to know now whether it was all over, and if Drew couldn't bring himself to tell her, she would tell him. She would end it.

She had been expecting that ending the relationship would bring a conclusion of sorts, but funnily enough although she had returned the ring and made her feelings plain, she didn't feel as if anything was concluded.

She knew why that was, of course. It was because Drew had said nothing, made no comment, given her no inclination of what his feelings were.

When she reached home, she telephoned Ellen, the office manager, and told her that she would not be coming in. She admitted to Ellen that she'd tripped and fallen against the door in the office yesterday evening, and that she was not feeling herself.

As she was up to date with all Drew's work, she was going to take it easy today.

There was absolutely no need to tell Ellen that she had already been in all the way to work and back again. Then she took two painkillers and went to bed.

5

'Football? What do you mean?' exclaimed Drew, standing on Zelma's front door-mat early on Saturday morning.

Robbie, who was standing on the other side of the doorway dressed in shorts and football socks and a long-sleeved striped jersey, looked puzzledly at Drew.

'What I said,' he told Drew patiently. 'I've got football.'

'Football?' Drew repeated again. 'But I asked you if you could miss the game!'

'I know,' Robbie said, 'and I can't.'

'But why didn't you phone and tell me that yesterday? Why didn't you — '

Robbie shrugged. 'I'm sorry,' he said as an afterthought, as if it was expected of him to apologise although, in reality, he felt no remorse at all.

Drew sighed, a great big enormous sigh and dug his hands into the pockets of his jeans.

For a moment neither Robbie nor Drew said anything. Drew stared studiously at the doormat, but under his fingertips, in his pocket, he was fingering Alison's engagement ring.

He'd put it there to keep her close to him, and he'd put it there in case he had a sudden and unexpected opportunity to return it to her.

Robbie stared at Drew. He was holding his breath, but he didn't want Drew to know that. Finally, when he thought his chest might burst, he said in a rush, 'Would you like to come in. Zelma's making scones.'

Drew shrugged. 'I suppose I'll have to,' he said.

Zelma's kitchen was in its usual shambles, only this time the kitchen table was miraculously clear of newspapers. A half-finished scrabble game sat on its wooden surface.

Zelma, up to her elbows in flour not clay this time, glanced at Drew as he came in the door. Her lips were pursed, Drew noted, as if they'd already said far too much, and she was banging out scones with the cutter as if they were heavy clods of earth.

The dogs clustered nervously around Drew as he sat down, and nosed his hands as if seeking protection. Drew patted first one head and then the other and talked gently to them, calming both himself and them, and wondering all the while what had been said to make them so jittery.

'What time is the game?' Drew asked.

He pulled the nearest rack of scrabble letters toward himself as a distraction, determined not to think about Alison. What had happened with Alison was surely just a glitch, once the weekend was safely behind him, he would come clean and everything would be restored, including the ring, to the way it was.

Hopefully even better than the way it was. Because, of course, he would have bonded with Robbie. In the meantime, he was going to try his utmost not to dwell on Alison. Although the anguished expression she'd worn on her face when she'd put the ring on his desk and he'd just sat there, stupid and dumbstruck, was very hard to get out of his mind.

'The game's in ten minutes,' Zelma said, as if she was now, finally, in a position to trust herself to speak. Then, 'Try the other one,' she said. 'Those letters are Robbie's.'

Zelma's letters were easier, Drew saw. She, at least, had two vowels, Robbie didn't have any. He glanced at the board and then he looked back down at her rack of letters. Vaguely in the background, aside from Zelma thumping out scones, he could hear somebody brushing their teeth.

'I'm ready,' Robbie said, appearing in the kitchen a minute later. Drew looked at him and put down a word, a word he thought indicative of the state of his life. The word was *chaos*.

'Drew,' Zelma said, wiping her hands on her shirt. 'Will you take Robbie to the game? I think if I have to I might strangle him along the way.'

Robbie, who was reaching over to put down a word on the scrabble board too, said nothing.

'Of course,' Drew said, standing up. 'Where to?'

'Brighton High School,' Robbie told him. He pulled his football jersey sleeves down so that they completely covered his fingers and, without a glance at his grandmother, went gingerly down the passage in his football boots.

'Robbie,' Drew said sharply, not moving.

Robbie waited until he was at the front door before he responded monosyllabically.

'Come back here,' Drew said.

Robbie came. He stood in the kitchen doorway and lolled against the frame, looking everywhere but at Drew and the scrabble board.

'Say goodbye to your grandmother,' Drew said.

Robbie smiled as if he'd been let off the hook.

'Goodbye Zel,' he said and cheekily blew her a kiss.

'Knock 'em dead,' Zelma told him, but she didn't smile back.

In the car on the way to the football game, Drew asked Robbie if Alison was likely to be there.

'Nuh,' Robbie said.

He tried again. He said, 'What's your mother doing then, this weekend?'

'Dunno,' Robbie said. He was fiddling with the car radio, trying to find Triple J, the radio station that anybody with half an ear, according to Robbie, had to listen to.

Drew, who didn't mind Triple J in small bursts and invariably let Robbie listen, didn't interfere.

At the football game, Drew stood desultorily at the sidelines, alone because he knew none of the other parents, and trying not to dwell on the morning now gone to waste.

Australian Rules Football wasn't a game Drew was particularly interested in, possibly because he wasn't Australian born and hadn't been brought up to regard the game in the same way as the British do their football. But he knew enough to realise that Robbie was almost the star of the game, in spite of the leanness of his build and his big feet and the fact that he couldn't see where he was going most of the time because he needed a haircut.

Robbie had the ball more often than most of the other boys, and he played not only aggressively and with spirit, but seemed to have a strategy of sorts which the other boys were lacking.

By the time they returned to Zelma's, Robbie, mud-streaked, with his socks around his ankles and clutching a half-eaten pie topped with sauce, was being appraised by Drew with new eyes. Drew was also now fairly cheerful.

Robbie's team had won the game by quite a large margin, and it didn't, in the scheme of things, seem to matter quite so much anymore that they would be half-a-day behind their schedule.

Zelma's scones were ready to be

eaten, which was another reason to be cheerful, and while Drew waited for Robbie to shower and change, he ate four without compunction, all four with heaped spoons of strawberry jam and lashings of cream.

6

By mid-afternoon, when Drew and Robbie had walked only half the distance they were scheduled to and Robbie's feet were beginning to drag and it was starting to spitter, Drew had a searing pain in his chest. Silently, he berated himself for being greedy and for letting himself dwell on Alison again.

He was quite sure it was the combination of the two that'd given him indigestion. He berated the weather bureau, too, for getting it wrong. They'd said it was going to be fine all weekend.

Fine, my foot, Drew thought, as he pulled his parka hood over his head. They were a long way from shelter, and they were going to get wet, that was obvious. It should have been obvious to the weather bureau. Glaringly obvious.

Drew could see that it was going to

take Robbie a month of Sundays to climb the hill ahead of them. That was also obvious. On top of the hill shelter awaited, but they had to get there first.

'Come on, Robbie, gee up,' Drew said, trying to sound encouraging and glancing back at the boy.

In response Robbie sat down. In the wet grass at the side of the track.

'Don't do that!' Drew said. 'You'll get your jeans soaked.'

'So?' Robbie said.

He let his rucksack fall from his shoulders and then he leaned back against it, pushed his hands into his pockets and closed his eyes. Drew thought Robbie closed his eyes, but he couldn't really see through all that hair whether they were closed or open.

'I'm tired,' Robbie announced. 'And I'm hungry.'

Food, Drew thought, rummaging in his rucksack. Food. He pulled out a muesli bar.

'Here,' he said. 'Eat this.'

Robbie sat up and crossed his legs

and devoured the muesli bar with the appetite of a locust.

'Got any more?' he asked when he was done. He screwed up the wrapping and pitched it into the bushes.

'Don't do that.'

'What?'

'Throw your wrapper into the bush.'

Robbie shrugged. He held out his hand. 'More,' he demanded.

'Wrapper,' Drew said warningly.

Robbie drew himself up with agonising slowness and lurched into the bush.

'Here,' he said a minute later, pressing the wrapper into Drew's hand.

In return Drew passed over two more muesli bars.

Robbie unwrapped the first bar and stuck it between his teeth while he hoisted his pack over his shoulders.

'Come on,' he said, talking around the muesli bar to Drew. 'We haven't got all day.'

★   ★   ★

Back in Brighton it wasn't spittering at all. It was, in fact, quite sunny. In the garden, where it was sheltered, Zelma and Harry were each holding a glass of white wine. The two dogs were lying at their feet in the overlong grass.

Bees were buzzing pleasantly. In the bottlebrush at the fence line a huddle of bright red and green rosellas were squawking and fighting over its blossoms.

'It's this creeper,' Zelma said, pulling at an offending tendril with one hand. 'It just takes over.'

'Morning glory,' said Harry. 'Have you done anything at all with the garden since you moved here?'

'Good Lord, no,' Zelma said. 'I was waiting for it to kind of grow on me.'

Harry laughed and she joined in.

'Oh dear,' she said. 'I didn't mean literally, although that's what seems to be happening.'

'No, what I meant is that I wanted to have a feel for the garden before I started ripping things out. But as you can see I've been here two years now and I haven't done a thing. Time gets away. I thought that when I retired from teaching art I would have so much of it. But I seem to have less than ever.' She paused. 'Do you have time?' she said to Harry.

'Yes,' Harry said. 'I have too much time. But that's probably because I'm very organised.'

'I'm not,' Zelma declared.

'I've noticed,' Harry said quietly.

He moved to the middle of the back lawn and surveyed the mess and muddle of disintegrating trellises, creepers, over-grown shrubs and leggy petunias.

'I could help you,' he said. 'Fix it up, I mean.'

'Could you?' Zelma asked, hopefully.

'Of course. I could start with cutting back everything and pulling out the weeds . . . then we can look at it again and decide what you want to keep and what you don't. Some of your shrubs are worth keeping. You have a pretty camellia in that corner. It just needs some sun.'

'That would be wonderful,' Zelma said. 'I'd really, really like that.'

She swallowed the last of her wine and squared her shoulders. 'Now,' she said. 'I suppose I'd better start on this sculpture.'

'You don't sound very keen.'

'I'm not, it's work. This — ' she made a sweeping gesture at the garden ' — is much more fun.'

★ ★ ★

'Sit still,' Zelma said to Harry as he perched on a kitchen stool with his head held up.

'I can't,' Harry said. 'It's the wine talking.'

'Just another half-an-hour,' Zelma told him. 'Then if you don't mind lighting the fire in the living-room, you can pass out there on the sofa.'

'Pass out?' Harry said. 'Nobody's going to pass out.'

'You know what I mean.'

Zelma, concentrating on the wet

lump of clay before her and studying Harry over the top of her glasses, was quiet again.

'Do you have a little catnap after lunch?' Harry asked her, speaking with his head held quite still as he did so.

'I sleep when I'm tired,' Zelma said. 'I don't care if it's after lunch or when it is.'

'You are a free spirit, aren't you.'

'Oh yes. It drove Charlie to distraction, it did.'

'Charlie?'

'Charlie was Alison's father. He's been dead now ten years.'

She paused. After a minute she said, 'And you? How long has your wife been gone?'

'Jaime? Eight years.'

'Do you get lonely?'

'Yes,' Harry said simply. 'I do.'

'But don't you do things like play bowls and volunteer work?'

'It's not the same as sharing a home with someone.'

Harry paused.

'Do you?' he asked. 'Do you get lonely?'

'No,' Zelma said. 'I have too much to distract me and I like being alone . . . but I miss company, you know, like this, just nattering.'

She stood back and examined the lump of clay which was no longer a lump and now had the very definite shape of a skull, and then she peered at Harry.

'When will you start?' she said.

'Start what?' Harry said, moving his eyes to look anxiously at her.

'The garden.'

'Oh,' Harry said. 'Whenever you like. Tomorrow?'

★　★　★

When Harry woke up after his nap rain was splattering against the windows. He went into the kitchen where Zelma was still moulding clay, located the kettle under a newspaper and put it on.

'Tea?' he said.

'Yes, please,' Zelma said without looking at him. 'And be a dear and open the fridge and get me something to eat.'

Harry opened the fridge. 'What do you want?'

'I think there's some dolmades left . . . on that plate covered with tin foil.'

Harry drew out the plate.

'Help yourself,' Zelma said.

'No thank you,' Harry said. 'Can't stand the little blighters.'

Zelma began to laugh.

'You knew,' Harry said. 'Didn't you?'

'I had an idea.'

'Where's today's crossword?' Harry asked a minute later, pushing a mug of tea across to her and still smiling quietly to himself.

Zelma looked at Harry over the top of her glasses. She really did have the biggest brown eyes Harry had ever seen.

'Probably on my bed,' Zelma told him. 'I didn't get very far with Robbie around this morning.'

'I wonder how they're going?' Harry took a sip of his tea.

'I'm not thinking about it,' Zelma said firmly.

'May I?' Harry asked standing at the doorway.

'What? Get the crossword from my room? Of course. But enter at your own peril.'

Zelma's bedroom was not at all like her kitchen, Harry thought. The bed was made for a start, with a white doona cover and blue cushions scattered at its head. It was a large room for a bedroom, Harry decided, simply but tastefully furnished.

He stood for a moment, quite still, in the bedroom, unable to remember when last he'd been in a woman's bedroom, apart from Jaime's. And, well, that was different, he'd shared the bedroom with Jaime and Jaime had been his wife.

This was something else, being in Zelma's room, a not unpleasant feeling, in fact, quite the reverse. Intimate, he thought. Exciting, in a way.

The newspaper was lying on a Persian carpet at the foot of the bed. Harry retrieved it and couldn't help noticing a photograph of Alison and Robbie on Zelma's bedside table. Alison really was a very pretty girl, Harry thought. Not only pretty but so sweet natured with it. He wondered if Drew knew how lucky he was.

'Do you think they'll have children?' Zelma said when Harry returned to the kitchen.

Harry pulled out a chair.

'Oh, I do hope so,' he said, putting on his reading glasses and opening the paper. 'I don't have any grandchildren as you're probably aware.'

'You'll have Robbie, soon.'

'I'll have Robbie, but the point is rather whether Robbie will have me, isn't it?'

Zelma smiled at Harry.

'Strange,' she said. 'How you understand the teenage thing, but Drew,' she shook her head, 'he just doesn't seem to get it, does he?'

Drew was, at that precious moment, not 'getting' the teenage thing at all. What he was getting, was exasperated.

'The tip of this,' Drew said to Robbie, handing him a long silver tent pole, 'goes in that little hole at the other end of the tent. Now I want you to go into the tent, find that little hole and stick in this tent pole.'

Robbie examined the mass of tent at his feet.

Drew said, 'Are you sure you've never put up a tent before?'

'It's dark in there,' Robbie said. 'How'll I find it?'

'I'll hold this end open,' Drew said patiently. 'It should give you enough light to see.'

Dubiously, Robbie took the pole while Drew lifted the mass of tent. Robbie peered into the entrance.

'You sure about this?'

'Yes,' said Drew, gritting his teeth.

Robbie steeped into the tent opening.

Drew took a deep breath and looked over his shoulder. He wasn't going to watch, it was so painful, he couldn't bear it.

'There,' said Robbie triumphantly after a minute or two.

Drew looked. The boy had actually done it. In the growing dark he could just see the tip of the pole peeping through.

'Well done,' he said.

'Now what?' said Robbie, appearing at the entrance.

'Robbie,' Drew said politely because if he didn't talk politely he thought he might shout, 'you're supposed to be down that end holding up that pole. You don't think it's going to stay up by itself, do you?'

Robbie turned and looked back over his shoulder.

'It's managed this far, hasn't it?'

Satisfied, he stepped out of the tent entrance, catching his shoulder on the front flap as he did so. Swaying gracefully, the entire back of the tent quietly collapsed.

Drew stepped away from the tent and put his head into his hands.

Robbie, kicking at a stone, wandered away.

When Drew turned he was sitting on a log, trying to juggle pebbles.

'You do it,' Robbie said. 'I'll watch.'

Drew had been worried about the rain dampening the wood and making it impossible to light a fire, particularly since he hadn't brought the gas cooker after all. It had just been too much to carry. But the many large eucalyptus had kept the undergrowth dry and making the fire was much easier than he expected, and certainly a breeze compared to erecting the tent.

But then Drew had known that building and making the fire would be a success. Fires were fascinating and boys — men for that matter, too — never got tired of making and attending to them.

His only criticism of Robbie was Robbie's over-enthusiasm. He put the fire out the first time by smothering it with kindling, and he put the fire out again by putting on a large log when it was only just at the beginning stage.

If Robbie had had a father, or even a grandfather, he would have known how to look after a fire, and Drew kept reminding himself that it wasn't the boy's fault. He must make allowances. He must show the boy how it was done. And he did. But when Robbie put the fire out a third time, Drew shouted at him.

'Leave it alone!' he said.

They ate dinner in silence. Dinner was baked beans and bacon and freeze-dried peas and hot tea. Robbie said he didn't like tea, but he took some anyway, and drank it, Drew noted.

Drew was cleaning up after dinner when Robbie said, 'Where's my sleeping bag?'

'Good idea,' Drew told him. 'You can unpack them both and roll them out in the tent. They're tied — '

'I know where they are,' Robbie told him.

Drew left him to it. He put some more wood on the fire, tiredly took off his wet boots, rummaged in his rucksack for his hip flask and stuck his damp feet in front of the fire. Robbie did not reappear.

The fire died down. It began to rain harder. Drew made sure the fire was properly out and brushed his teeth, feeling totally miserable and spitting into his mug. He had less than a day to make this bonding thing with Robbie work. How could you accomplish anything in less than a day? Particularly if it was going to pour with rain.

In the tent, the rain was pattering on the roof and Robbie was quietly snoring. He'd taken his trainers off, they were outside the tent entrance, but so far as Drew could tell, he was still fully dressed.

Drew pulled his trainers inside so that they didn't get wet, took off his parka and his jeans, and folded them at the bottom of his sleeping bag. Then he quietly unzipped the bag, snuggled himself inside it and lay back.

He thought lovingly of Alison and wondered what she was doing, and how she would feel alongside him in a sleeping bag. She was so little, she wouldn't take up much space. They hadn't yet done any camping trips together. It was possible, Drew thought hopelessly, that they might never do any camping trips together. It was possible that —

Suddenly he sniffed. Something didn't smell right. He sat up and wriggled his hips in the sleeping bag. Then he felt the sleeping bag between his fingers. The material was a little bit crisp on the outside and stiff on the inside. He had the wrong bag. This was the new one, smelling distinctly new.

He gazed over at Robbie, now just a lump in the dark. Robbie, who'd decided that the old sleeping bag must be meant for him, that the new one naturally must belong to Drew, and he felt a sudden and unfamiliar surge of warmth for the boy.

7

Alison was having a nightmare. She shouted, and her shouting woke her. Breathless, she sat up and peered at her alarm clock. It was five-thirty. Closing her eyes, she lay back down again and snuggled under the covers.

She'd been dreaming of Robbie. They were on a boat for some reason, a sort of ocean cruiser, and something was wrong, the boat was sinking she thought. In any event, Robbie was trying to push her out of the cabin window. She was resisting because she didn't have a lifejacket. But he was oddly gleeful.

She remembered him shouting, words he wouldn't use in real life, 'Go on, Mum, take the plunge. Don't worry about me.' And then he pushed her out of the window into the sea!

And suddenly (as these things happen

in dreams) the cruiser was a building several storeys high and an awful, awful long way from the ocean and she was falling and falling . . .

She shuddered and kicked her legs up and down under the blankets. What a ratbag Robbie was to throw her out of the window! But how she loved him, how she missed him when he was away.

Thoroughly awake now, she decided to get up. She was feeling better than she had been feeling the day before. Saturday had been the most miserable of days. It had rained most of the afternoon and all of the night, and she had cried along with the rain.

She'd wished her mother hadn't chosen that particular weekend, out of all weekends, to want Robbie. It would have distracted her to have Robbie around. It would have stopped her crying, not altogether, but not quite so much. And she might have eaten something sensible, instead of just half a bar of chocolate.

She had been tempted to phone

Zelma just to talk, not to want to see or interfere with the sculpture, she knew better than that. But sometimes her mother was a little bit strange when she was working, abrupt and to-the-point, and Alison, in no state for abrupt and to-the-point, decided against it.

Also, she'd made a decision not to tell anyone about Drew yet, and speaking to her mother, she knew, might very well undo that decision.

She had decided not to tell anybody about Drew because it all seemed surreal. She couldn't quite comprehend that the man she'd thought was different had turned out to be the same as all the other men.

In her heart of hearts she was sure there must be some mistake, something that would exonerate Drew and return him to her where he belonged. And she felt that if she waited long enough — not too long you understand, just long enough — it would magically all come right.

She pushed her curtains away from

the window, but it was still too dark to see what kind of day it was going to be, although there did appear to be one or two stars about.

In the kitchen she made herself tea to start with and later she ate two soft poached eggs on toast, with lots of salt and pepper, the way she liked them. But then she could tell it was going to be a nice but cold day, no more rain at any rate, and she made a pact with herself. As long as the rain kept away, she would ensure the tears did, too.

She picked a couple of camellias from her garden and wrapped the stems in tin foil and then got dressed, choosing a pretty pink lipstick to detract from the bruised bags under her eyes.

* * *

'Alison!' her sister-in-law said to her an hour later. 'But I thought you weren't coming.'

Alison moved into the slightly gloomy

hallway of Liz's home, pushing the camellias into Liz's hand, and taking off her coat.

'I thought so, too, but I couldn't bear another minute of my own company.'

'Now let me get this straight,' Liz said. 'Drew is away at a conference, and Robbie is at your mother's all week-end?'

'Yes,' said Alison, nodding, relieved to get that all behind her.

'Hooley Dooley,' said Liz, 'the man got something right!'

'Talking of Greg, where is he?' Alison asked, following Liz down the passage. The house was unusually quiet.

'You won't believe this, but he's taken Liam and Patrick to the football. Only Stephen and I are here.'

Liz turned to her as they entered the family room.

'Oh, I'm so glad you've come,' she said with warmth. 'It will be lovely to have some time to ourselves.'

She stopped and frowned at Alison.

'But what have you done to your

face?' she asked. 'Why are your eyes so baggy?'

'Oh, I've got some, um, allergy,' Alison told her, loosely gesturing in the air and not looking at her sister-in-law. She'd worked that out in the car. 'My whole face just puffed up . . . and I can't wear make-up at the moment, just lipstick.'

She wasn't really lying. She did have an allergy. She was presently allergic to Drew. And she couldn't wear make-up because crying made her mascara run.

'Stephen!' she said, catching sight of a little boy sitting bolt upright on the carpet about a metre from the television.

Stephen was the only one of her nephews who looked remotely like Robbie. He had that same thatch of dark brown hair, and he was small and wiry like Robbie had been at the same age.

He turned sideways, eyed her solemnly and silently with big brown eyes then turned away again.

'Stevie,' she said, warningly to his back.

But he took no notice.

Alison, tiptoeing, advanced upon him, caught him under the arms of his little striped yellow and blue T-shirt and swung him into the air.

'Arghh,' he said, and then he started to laugh. Alison loved his laugh. The sound of it always made her very happy. It was like a chuckling, tinkling stream, and he could break it off and start again, at will it seemed. When he stopped laughing, she tickled him and made him laugh again . . . and again until Liz said, 'Alison!'

When she put Stevie down, her sister-in-law was looking at her in an exasperated way.

'Sorry,' Alison said meekly.

But Stevie was now completely wound up. There was no stopping him. Roaring like a steam train going full tilt up a hill, he raced from the family room down the passage to the front of the house and back again, his arms pumping at his sides.

On his second lap, Alison caught him and held him close. He struggled, kicking her shins, clawing her hands and bucking his head, but she murmured softly to him until, eventually, he was still.

Then, 'Stevie,' she said, 'Mummy says you have a new story book. Can I read it to you? Please?'

When Liz brought the coffee over on a tray, they were on their second reading of the book.

Stephen was on Alison's lap, his back resting quietly against her chest, his head quite still under her moving chin.

Alison, glancing up at Liz, as she turned the page, saw Liz's mouth moving.

'Washing,' Liz said in a stage whisper, 'just going to hang up the washing . . .'

Alison nodded. She began to read again

'The boy picked up Leonard and held him to his chest so tightly that Leonard thought he'd never be able to

breathe again. 'I thought I'd lost you,' the boy scolded, looking at the soft toy, the little lion with the bent tail who was a coward and who was really alive. 'I thought you'd gone for ever. I . . . ' '

Alison trailed off.

Stevie moved his head from her chest and looked at her.

'Why are you crying?' he asked curiously.

'Because . . . because it's . . . it's so sad,' Alison got out. 'It's so aw-awfully sad.'

'Don't cry. Please,' Stevie said, staring hard at the tears glistening on her cheeks.

He put a finger up to her face and touched it, and then he took his finger away and examined the wetness shining at its tip.

He got off her lap. 'I'll b'ing you a tissue,' he said.

Alison, struggling to get herself under control, watched Stevie manfully drag a chair across to a chest of drawers, launch himself on to its seat, stagger precariously upright and then reach across a minefield of precious ornaments for the tissue box.

She knew that what had made her cry wasn't the story of the little boy with the soft toy called Leonard. What had made her cry was the act of holding Stevie's small and warm body to her chest.

It had induced a very definite desire, a desire culminating in certain knowledge, knowledge that she wanted another baby. Not just anybody's baby.

She wanted Drew's baby.

Rising from the sofa, she caught Stevie in a big hug before he could begin his descent, and before she could begin to cry again.

'Thank you, Stevie,' she said, swallowing and drying her eyes with the proffered tissue. 'Thank you.'

She knew that she was thanking him not only for the tissue. She was thanking him for something which she hadn't, before now, clarified in her own mind.

She and Drew had never discussed having children. Alison wasn't sure why. Probably because of Robbie, she imagined. Probably because Drew hadn't wanted to put her under any sort of pressure; he was kind like that.

She took a deep breath. This desire to marry Drew and to have his baby suddenly now seemed the most exciting knowledge, certainly the most treasured knowledge in the world and, more than anything, she wanted to tell him.

But she couldn't, could she. It was over between them. She, Alison Whitehead, had taken matters into her own hands and ended it. Or was it over? Could she do something about the rift between them? Perhaps it was a case of a simple misunderstanding? Had she been too hasty in giving Drew his ring back?

If only there was some way to reclaim the ring, she thought, to retrieve it without Drew knowing. But that was silly. How could Drew not know?

When Liz returned from hanging up

the washing, Alison and Stevie were reading a Dr Seuss book and giggling at the sketches as if nothing untoward had ever taken place.

But that night, long after Alison had gone home and Greg and Stevie's brothers had got back from the game, when Liz was putting Stephen to bed he was unusually quiet. He was also sucking his thumb, which he rarely did these days since his brothers teased him unmercifully if they caught him at it.

'Are you OK?' his mother gently asked as she tucked the covers under his chin.

He took his thumb out of his mouth and considered it. 'Do you cry sometimes?' he asked.

'Sometimes,' Liz repeated. She thought sometimes was a big word for Stevie.

'Why?' she asked him.

'Auntie Ali was crying today.'

'Was she now?' she said, touching the tip of his nose. 'When?'

'When we read.' He put his thumb back into his mouth.

'Was the story sad?'

He shook his head.

'Nuh,' he said. 'She was sad.'

'Is that right?'

Liz leaned forward and kissed his cheek. 'Well, sometimes people do get sad,' she said. 'It's just part of life.'

She moved to the doorway and turned off the light. 'Night-night,' she said.

'Mum,' he said, suddenly sitting bolt upright. 'Don't go.'

'Oh Stevie,' she said tiredly. 'What now?'

'Jus' sit,' he told her, pointing to the chair.

She sat on the easy chair next to his bed, a chair which had been placed alongside Stevie's bed specifically for sitting in until he was asleep. He closed his eyes.

She closed her eyes too, and then shook her head to open them again. She mustn't fall asleep. If she did, she would forget what Stevie had said. Sometimes. It was, she thought, his first big abstract word, and she wanted to remember it so that she could share it with Greg.

Greg said, 'Ah,' when Liz appeared, blinking like an owl after the darkness of Stevie's room.

'Ah, what?' she asked, but he didn't say anything, just took her hand and led her on to the wooden deck adjoining their family room.

Outside the skies were clear but as a result it was crisp and cold. So cold that Liz could see her breath in front of her face, but she didn't complain, she was too intrigued.

She let Greg ease her into the cushioned rattan sofa, and she let him wrap a mohair rug around her shoulders without uttering so much as a why? or a what?

But when he reached for a bottle of champagne, popped the cork and poured her a glass, she was almost beside herself with curiosity.

'To us,' Greg said, clinking his glass gently against hers.

'To us,' she repeated, now on the edge of her seat.

Greg slid on to the sofa beside her and took her hand.

'I was going to start off by asking if you want the good news first or the bad news,' he said, 'but it isn't really like that.' He paused. 'I mean there is good news but — '

'Could you just get to the point?' Liz said, interrupting.

Greg took another gulp of his champagne. Liz waited. He said, 'It's not easy ... I've been putting it off ... for days. I don't know which bit to tell you first.'

'Start with the easiest bit,' she said, putting down her champagne. 'What's the least difficult part to tell me?'

'I've been promoted,' Greg admitted.

'Oh,' Liz said, turning to him with shining eyes and picking up her glass again and clinking it against his.

'Oh Greg, that's wonderful. Congratulations,' she told him, leaning over and kissing him on the cheek.

'Liz,' he blurted out. 'They want me to go to England.'

'I know that,' she said. 'You're leaving at the end of this week.'

'Yes,' he said quietly, holding his champagne glass in his hand but not drinking any of it. 'I'm leaving at the end of this week,' he repeated.

He took a gulp, and looked hard at her.

'They want me to go for six months,' he said. 'It's a trial thing. If it goes OK, I may get offered a contract for two years. If I don't I'll come home again and everything will be just as it was before.'

'Six months?' Liz said. She put down her champagne with an unsteady hand, pulled the mohair rug tighter around her shoulders, and began to pick at its fringe.

When she'd married Greg, he'd been a sports journalist and she'd known what the position had entailed, known that he'd be away for weeks at a time, and that he'd miss out on huge chunks of her life. But that was then, when they didn't have children, and this was now, and she didn't think she could carry on accepting that this was how it was always going to be.

'Liz,' he said, quietly, meaningfully.

But she lowered her head and refused to look at him.

'I want you to come with me,' Greg said. 'I want us all to go. I don't want us to be apart anymore.'

8

The next morning when Drew woke up it was still pouring with rain, and it had got very cold as the teacher in the school playground had said it could.

Drew felt as if he'd only been asleep for five minutes. This was due to his mind insisting on waking every couple of hours to check whether it was still raining, which it was, and his back keeping up a continuous protest at the lack of adequate support.

They would have to have a cold breakfast, he thought with distaste. There was no chance of getting a fire to light. Robbie would be disappointed. Drew was disappointed too, at the thought of cold tinned food . . . when all he really wanted was a mug of hot, steaming coffee.

But the rain didn't seem to make any difference to Robbie. He carried on as if it wasn't raining. He even tried to make a fire.

'Can we make it in the tent?' he asked, when, after his third attempt, it failed to light.

Drew wanted to say, 'Are you crazy!' but instead said, 'The wood's wet, Robbie. It wouldn't make any difference where you made it.'

Robbie kicked at the wet twigs, scattering them.

'What's for breakfast?'

'Cold muffins,' Drew told him.

'Got any jam?'

Drew shook his head.

'Muesli bars?'

'A couple.'

Robbie held out his hand. 'Please,' he said making it a statement more than a request.

By eight they were on their way, the soggy tent making Drew's pack very heavy. By contrast, his stomach felt very light. He'd eaten a muffin but he was wary of another. They were inclined to be doughy when cold and the last thing he wanted was another attack of indigestion.

Robbie had eaten all the muesli bars for breakfast and chugged back the last tin of soft drink. Drew had only brought two, both for Robbie. He knew how important it was to keep him hydrated.

Drew had, of course, planned on having hot coffee, and he knew he should at least have a drink of cold water, but he couldn't face it. Not just yet, maybe when he'd warmed up.

Robbie had seemed surprisingly cheerful, Drew thought, and open to conversation, if only he could think of something interesting to say.

They trudged down the tree-lined track in silence, both with their hoods on and their hands in their pockets because it was cold. They were high up on a hill, sheltered from the elements by the trees for the moment, but Drew knew that soon they would leave the trees behind them, and come out into the rain proper and the salt-laden wind blowing up from the sea.

That section of the journey was normally quite spectacular. A sharp fall of cliff to the left of the track, then the sea some distance below, rising up and crashing against the rocks. To the right, low scrub and bush, then green forests, and finally rolling hills dotted with farmhouses at the horizon. On a calm and sunny day the view was enough to take your breath away.

Today, as Drew discovered, it was the wind that took his breath away. As they grew close to the edge of trees lining the path, Drew felt the force of the wind stirring. They came out into the open with the sea on their left, and the wind roared up from the sea and lifted the hood of his parka and blew it back. It stung his cheeks and his ears and made his nose run.

Robbie, who was already wearing his knitted cap, kept going without pausing, but Drew, staggering for a moment under his load and the push of the wind, stopped. He needed to find his cap, but he couldn't remember where he'd put it.

He swung his rucksack off his back, but it was heavier than he thought because of the tent, and he almost overbalanced before he got it safely down on to the ground. Shocked, he peered anxiously over the cliff edge to the crashing waves on the rocks below.

On his haunches, he began to unbuckle the pack, but he realised, foolishly, that out in the open as he was, was not the place to begin a search for a knitted cap. The wind lifted the rucksack's cover and peered inquisitively inside, and threatened to take several items over the cliff's edge.

Still on his haunches, on the narrow path, he did up the pack again. His windswept head and freezing ears would just have to wait. He glanced over his shoulder to see where Robbie had got to, and saw that he had covered quite some distance. Obviously he'd assumed, not unreasonably, that Drew would catch him up.

Drew, realising that it was his turn to gee up, felt the force of the wind rock his body as he quickly rose. Lifting the heavy pack and staggering slightly, he gave it a good swing to get it over his shoulder.

Unbelievably and quite suddenly, his vision blurred and his knee trembled.

He shook his head. But the thought registered, passing through his mind fleetingly, that he'd had no liquid and very little food.

And that he'd also just stood up in a hurry. It would be so silly, he thought, so awfully stupid in fact, if, like Alison, he fainted.

★ ★ ★

It was some time before Robbie realised that Drew was not trudging alongside him, that he had not caught up to him.

He stopped, turned and looked back, shielding his face against the rain. But he couldn't see Drew further back or along the path at all. Through the mist and the rain he could see the line of trees where they'd come out into the open and he could follow most of the track, except for one or two places where it suddenly dropped away and there was a pile of rocks, but he couldn't see Drew.

He bent his back and retraced his steps, trudging up the hill, looking off to the left every now and again to see if Drew was anywhere in the shrubs, for the call of nature.

When he reached the place where they'd exited from the trees and he still hadn't found Drew, he knew he'd been fooling himself about Drew being in the shrubs. He turned around and looked back down the hill. The greenery was all bushy, low stuff and it was not possible to hide in it or even lie in it without being seen.

He walked down a bit to the place where he thought Drew had stopped. He'd been aware that Drew had stopped. He knew that Drew had needed his knitted cap without being told. It was obvious. What he couldn't understand was why Drew hadn't thought of his cap before they'd left the camp site earlier. He shook his head. Grown-ups were an inexplicable lot sometimes.

He sat down, as he'd done yesterday, at the side of the path and in the rain. So where could Drew be? He put up his hand again to shield his face from the rain, and he saw something shining dully in the grass at the edge of the cliff.

He peered at it, but it was only an old soft drink can, flattened by someone's boot. Co-incidentally, the brand was the same as the one he'd had for breakfast. Shrugging off his backpack, he leaned forward and crawled over the muddy track to retrieve the can.

He picked up the can in one hand and, leaning on the other, peeped cautiously over the edge of the cliff. Heights were thrilling, but Robbie wasn't too sure he liked them.

A long way down, the sea roared and

bucked against the rocks below, a foaming mass of suds like washing-up water, Robbie thought.

He withdrew his head and moved backwards to the safety of his rucksack. And in that split second when he pulled his head back and he was no longer concentrating on the sea, he saw a bit of a narrow ledge, jutting out from the cliff, about halfway down. A boot was on that bit of ledge, a boot which was fixed to a leg. A jeaned leg.

He reached the safety of his rucksack and wondered if he was hallucinating.

He scrambled forward on his hands and knees again and lowered himself to his stomach near the cliff's edge, inching slowly forwards. After he'd pushed the wet hair out of his eyes and tucked it into his cap, he saw that the boot and leg belonged to a body.

The body was spread-eagled on the narrow ledge, a backpack cushioning its fall, and one of its legs caught awkwardly behind the other. When he eventually permitted his gaze to look at the face on the body, he saw that the face belonged to Drew.

Robbie had to inch back to his backpack and sit up straight before he could think clearly. Leaning over the edge of an abyss on your stomach with the wind in your face, peering at a body — a body! — was enough to make anyone feel nauseous. Particularly since the body belonged to somebody he knew.

Robbie's first instinct was to run all the way down the hill to the ranger's hut. He knew where the ranger's hut was, they'd passed it on their way into the Park, but Robbie wasn't sure if running all the way down the hill would bring him there. He could still get lost when he reached the bottom.

So, he marked off on one finger, that was one problem.

The second problem he marked off on a second finger, was that he shouldn't — couldn't — leave Drew until he knew whether he was injured and just unconscious or whether

. . . whether he was . . . whether he was . . .

Robbie couldn't complete the thought.

In the steady rain, he emptied out the entire contents of his backpack on the grass in front of him and picked out the things he thought he would need, the new sleeping bag Drew had given him as a present that morning, his water bottle, and his penknife, just in case.

He took off his parka and left that on the ground. It would just be a nuisance. Throwing the rucksack over his shoulders, he fastened it securely around his middle so that it didn't bump around on his back. Then he made his way forward on his hands and knees to the edge of the cliff again.

Robbie had done abseiling at school just a few months ago. It wasn't a school camp, just a leadership course, a one-day thing. He'd enjoyed it immensely, although he wasn't generally good with heights.

He learned at the course that if he didn't look down or into the distance, and only concentrated on finding a foothold for one foot after another, he was absolutely fine. In fact, he was better than a lot of the other boys and girls who had no fear of heights.

Of course abseiling wasn't the same as climbing down a cliff face unassisted. But he didn't see why it should be so terribly different. He tried it now. Not looking below him, he swung one foot over the edge and felt with it for a small rocky outcrop of some kind where he could safely balance his body weight. Once he had achieved this, he swung the rest of his body over.

He had one near disaster. His foot slipped off a rock which was smooth and particularly slippery from the rain. He cried out, but didn't fall. The root of a shrub which he gripped fiercely in his right hand saved him, and he sent up a prayer to shrubs and their roots and vowed to pay more attention to his mother's garden from now on.

When he reached Drew his legs were trembling and he was soaked through, with sweat and with rain. He had to be very careful on the ledge with Drew because it was very narrow, and with Drew's body taking up most of the space, he had to watch where he put his feet.

He tried to find Drew's pulse by feeling his wrist, but he didn't really know what he was looking for and wasn't surprised when he couldn't find it.

He stared at Drew, who lay very still looking like Drew, but also not looking like Drew. Watching him, Robbie couldn't detect whether he was breathing, his parka was too bulky for Robbie to see whether his chest moved up and down or not.

But he didn't look dead, Robbie decided, not that he'd ever seen a dead person. On the ground, at the back of Drew's head, a pool of blood had spread, and the awkwardly placed leg was just that. Awkwardly placed. Broken, perhaps, Robbie thought.

Leaning over, grimacing, he laid his head on Drew's chest. there was nothing but the howl of the wind, the sound of the waves breaking below and the rain which had eased to a patter on his cheek. He pushed down harder.

And there it was! A heartbeat. Faint, very faint, but there. Robbie raised his head and smiled.

He undid his backpack, and drew out the sleeping bag. He unzipped it and covered Drew with it, tucking it underneath his arms and the boot of the good leg so that it wouldn't blow away. Ferreting in the backpack again, he drew out his water bottle.

He knew that he shouldn't touch or move Drew in case he'd hurt his back, but he really needed to know how to get to the ranger's hut.

'Drew,' he said urgently, bending over him and letting some water dribble into his mouth which was slightly open.

Drew made a gagging sound and coughed. Robbie, suddenly paralysed with the fear that he'd choked him, held his breath. But then he saw Drew swallow, and he let the air out of his lungs in a big rush.

'Drew,' he said again, loudly this time. Drew opened his eyes.

'Here,' Robbie said, tapping his finger agitatedly on his chest because Drew seemed to be having trouble focusing. His eyes were wandering all over the place.

'It's me, Robbie,' Robbie said.

Drew tried to lift his head.

'No,' Robbie told him, placing his palm over his forehead. 'Stay here. You can't move.'

'Where am I?' Drew said weakly.

'On a ledge,' Robbie said. 'You fell. Can you wriggle your toes?' He remembered this from some emergency hospital programme he'd watched on television.

Robbie saw the good boot move, but the leg caught underneath remained motionless.

Drew's hand appeared from under the sleeping bag. It was shaking a little. Robbie took it and held it between his own. It was very cold.

'How did you get here?'

'Climbed,' Robbie said.

Drew closed his eyes . . .

'Wait,' Robbie said frantically. 'I need to know how to get to the ranger's hut.'

'Ranger's hut?' Drew repeated, but he was slurring his words.

'Yes, it's important.'

Robbie, kneeling at Drew's side, glanced back at the cliff behind him. He was going to have to climb back up that cliff. He wasn't sure whether he could.

'Down, not up,' Drew murmured.

'What?' Robbie said, but Drew said nothing.

'Drew,' Robbie said loudly, but Drew didn't respond.

What did he mean, down not up?

Robbie looked frustratedly at him and then, on an impulse pushed back one of Drew's eyelids.

'Drew!' he demanded.

Underneath the eyelid, a white matter bulged, looking grotesque. The actual eye, like Drew, seemed to have withdrawn.

'Ugh,' Robbie said, and jerked his hand away.

9

It was only when Robbie, almost crying with frustration and his fingers numb and bleeding, had given up trying to scale the cliff, that the significance of Drew's words dawned upon him.

Down, not up. Why had Drew told him that? There must be a reason.

Perhaps, down below, there was a path, a path just before the cliff fell into the sea?

Robbie had no way of finding out. He had no room to squirm forward on his tummy and peer over the edge; And there was no way he could stand and look over the edge. That was too dangerous. He'd done that at the leadership camp and had to go and sit down on a rock. He had to believe that Drew knew what he was talking about Down, not up. He had to trust Drew.

He hadn't, up until now, trusted

Drew at all. He knew that. He also knew that he'd got some perverse pleasure out of not trusting Drew, and out of behaving in the exact opposite manner that his mother and Drew wanted.

But perhaps it was time to stop all that. Or, at least to stop it for the time being. Drew was, after all, unconscious and some sort of grown-up behaviour was called for here. His own behaviour to date, Robbie had to admit, was also becoming rather tiresome.

As an example, he'd rather like to have a hair cut. His hair was a nuisance this length and he was really quite over having it long.

This time he couldn't lever himself over the edge on his tummy, there was no space. Balancing on his hands and knees, on the edge of the cliff, on a very minute patch of rocky ground on the sea side of Drew, he pushed his right leg down and again felt cautiously for some little bulge of stone to test with his foot, and then to lower his weight on to.

A toasted sandwich steamed fragrantly on a plate in the ranger's hut. It had been made with wholegrain bread, real butter, a thick slice of genuine ham — none of that thin supermarket stuff tasting like water — a wedge of Brie cheese and French mustard.

The ranger, who was young and lived alone, liked being inventive with his meals. He also believed that a meal was an occasion and should be thoughtfully prepared and eaten with some ceremony.

He'd just put the side plate on his desk alongside his computer, moved the heater a little closer, gone back for a paper napkin, when the door burst open letting in a blast of cold air and a scattering of raindrops.

'What — ' he said in surprise.

A boy, puffing and heaving with exertion, came to a halt against the door frame. Underneath the dirt the Ranger could see that the boy's face

144

was very pale and almost blue with cold, and the pupils of his large brown eyes were dilated.

What's more, he was soaked through. Water dripped off the thin T-shirt he wore and puddled on to the floor.

'Help . . . ' the boy panted at him.

★   ★   ★

Robbie popped the last bite of the toasted sandwich into his mouth and licked his fingers. The ranger watched enviously.

'Awesome,' Robbie said, peering round the crudely furnished dwelling as if toasted sandwiches of the quality he'd just eaten had to be made by a white-aproned chef hiding in a stainless steel kitchen.

'Got any more?'

'No,' the ranger said abruptly, taking Robbie's plate.

He glanced down at Robbie sitting on the sofa in front of the heater, not quite believing that this underfed boy with overlong hair had descended a cliff and run ten kilometres as he claimed.

'If you're feeling strong enough I'll need you to come with us in the helicopter, so you can show me where this friend of yours is.'

'Sweet,' Robbie said, rising from the sofa, clutching the blanket he'd been given around himself. 'When do we go?'

'Sit down,' the ranger said, pushing Robbie back down on to the sofa. 'Not for some time, I'm afraid. It will take at least an hour for the chopper to get here.'

'An hour?' Robbie said incredulously. He tried to rise again. This time he succeeded in evading the ranger's hand, and quickly moved out of reach to the other side of the heater.

'Drew can't wait that long,' he said.

The ranger knew that the rescue helicopter's schedule was stretched. It was a sad fact, but other national parks had priority, and in spite of repeated requests the ranger was seldom given any credence. Though an accident such as this boy was claiming, would help his cause enormously.

'There's nothing we can do,' the ranger said brusquely.

'We could make more sandwiches,' Robbie said hopefully.

The ranger gave him a grim look and disappeared.

But while he was gone, Robbie stopped thinking of melted cheese and thick ham between crunchy, buttered pieces of hot toast. Instead he thought about Drew. He didn't want to, but it happened.

Drew lying on a narrow ledge in the cold and the rain. Drew wafting in and out of consciousness. Drew's leg lying at an odd angle, the blood pooling behind his head. And then an image of his mother's face floated into his mind, his mother's face when she heard about Drew.

Picking up the shirt and jeans the ranger had produced for him to wear, he held them up against his now dry body for size.

When the ranger returned with two plates of sandwiches, Robbie was dressed. Helping himself to both halves from one of the plates, he bit into one half.

'I'm going now,' he said to the ranger with his mouth full.

'Going?'

'Yup,' he said. 'I can't leave Drew while we wait for the helicopter.'

'You can't go,' the ranger said emphatically, at the same time wondering how he would stop the kid.

'I need you,' he told Robbie. 'I need you to show me where this friend of yours is.'

Earlier the ranger had asked Robbie if Drew was his father, but Robbie had said no, Drew was his friend, he didn't have a father. This admission had made the ranger feel a little uncomfortable, as if he should put his arm around Robbie and say something deep and meaningful.

Now Robbie said, 'But I've told you where he is.'

He bit fiercely into the other half of

the toasted sandwich. For some reason this second one didn't taste as nice as the first one had.

The ranger said nothing.

'You can't stop me,' Robbie said, again with his mouth full.

'And if I go now, I can be there long before you, and I can wave when I see you. That way you won't miss us.'

The ranger studied Robbie's empty plate, then narrowed his eyes. He felt awful posing the question, but it had to be asked. 'But what if — '

'But what if what?' Robbie demanded, chewing.

The ranger said nothing.

'I know what you're thinking,' Robbie said, swallowing. 'What if I'm lying? Right?'

From under bushy eyebrows the ranger looked silently at Robbie, not denying the question, just as he couldn't deny the possibility that it might all be a hoax.

'You'll just have to trust me,' Robbie said.

At the door, he began to pull on his trainers, which were cold and wet and difficult to get on.

'People have to trust each other, you know,' he told the ranger in a worldly tone, looking over his shoulder at him. 'It's a fact of life.'

10

For reasons best known only to Harry, reasons which Harry couldn't probably put into words but which existed nonetheless, he was still at Zelma's when the phone rang on Sunday evening.

Zelma, who was sitting across the kitchen table from Harry with the few remaining crossword clues he'd unselfishly left her, quite liked seeing him there. In the space of two days she'd got accustomed to having him around, and oddly enough wasn't in any sort of hurry for him to go home.

The rain had stopped pelting down as if out of control though, and she was aware that she couldn't use that as an excuse for him to stay any longer. She couldn't use the sculpture as an excuse either, because that was sitting on the table between her and Harry, looking remarkably like Robbie.

She wondered why it had taken her so long to get to know Harry. He talked about interesting things, did Harry, and he was useful. He did things like clearing out fireplaces and making tea and walking dogs.

And then there were his looks because, like his son, he was easy on the eye. It was true that his hair was thinning, but his body was in good shape and his pale-blue eyes were attentive, so that when he was speaking or listening to you, you knew he wasn't thinking about other things like cricket scores or stocks and bonds, as other men did.

Zelma, who was closest to the phone when it rang, picked it up.

Harry continued to read his newspaper. It was only after Zelma said 'Really!' and looked concernedly at Harry, a look which he rather warmed to, that Harry began to eavesdrop.

'No!' she exclaimed to the caller, and then 'When?' and looked at her watch.

'Are you OK?' she asked carefully. Then, a minute later, 'Oh yes,' nodding her head vigorously, 'Oh yes. Of course,' she said. At this point she looked at Harry over the top of her glasses and met his eyes.

Harry lowered his head, feeling discomfited by meeting Zelma's eyes but also pleasantly disturbed. It had been a long time since a woman had looked at him quite that way.

When she put the phone down without saying goodbye, saying instead, 'We'll see you soon,' she looked at Harry again over the top of her glasses and in her usual brusque way said, 'That was Robbie. Drew's fallen off the mountain.'

★　★　★

Harry thought that *Waiting Room* wasn't a very clever title. It gave no indication of the length of time one could be kept waiting. Sometimes, as in the case of Drew's birth — admittedly a

long time ago but still a vivid memory
— you could be there for whole days.
Other times — like now — they'd been
waiting two-and-a-half hours Harry
calculated.

By all accounts it was never quick,
the time spent waiting. Perhaps, Harry
reflected, a cleverer title would be
Interminable Waiting Room.

Alison was sitting between him and
Zelma. They were in a little country
hospital, on chairs with rusting steel
legs and worn laminated green seat
covers, all three of them were staring at
the blank wall opposite, and trying to
sip scalding hot tea from polystyrene
cups.

Zelma had her arm around Alison's
shoulders, and every now and again
Harry would feel Zelma's fingers
brushing against his arm, just letting
him know that she was there.

But Harry was calm. He knew that
Drew was OK, that the doctor was just
setting his leg and stabilising him, and
that although he was suffering from

exposure, his body was strong and in the young intern's words, he would soon come good.

Alison was calm in a different way. Her black shiny hair, which was normally swept off her face and caught up behind her head, was loose and curtained her face like a veil, and, unless you were looking at her straight on, it was very difficult to see her expression.

She was dressed entirely in black, from the boots on her small feet to the turtle-neck sweater, and she was terribly, terribly quiet. Harry doubted that she'd said two words the whole time they'd been waiting.

In the car, on the journey out to the hospital, she'd said virtually nothing. He'd expected her, at least, to rail against them both for keeping Drew and Robbie's secret from her, but she hadn't even done that.

Even when they'd been allowed to see Robbie, he recalled that Alison had said very little. With brimming eyes, she'd clutched the boy fiercely to her as if she would never let him go again.

Eventually, Robbie had said, 'Mum,' and gently extricated himself, but he clearly wasn't embarrassed by her attentions, which was wonderful Harry thought watching from the end of Robbie's bed, a lump rising in his throat. It was just that he couldn't breathe, poor kid.

Glancing at Alison sitting beside him, Harry thought that she was like a badly brewed bottle of home-made beer, that in an hour or a minute — there was no telling with home-brewed beer — she would explode and it would all come out, whatever it was she had bottled up inside.

And judging by the absence of her engagement ring on her finger, about which he'd tactfully said nothing, there was a powerful mixture bottled up inside.

The door to the *Interminable Waiting Room* suddenly opened and the young intern popped his head around it. He was smiling, which Harry thought odd considering the seriousness of the whole matter, smiling as if something quite amusing had just happened which he couldn't possibly share with them.

'You can see Mr Stephenson now,' he said, trying hard to straighten his face. 'But only one at a time. And not for long.'

Alison looked questioningly at Harry, but Harry gave her a gentle push and said, 'There's no question about it, off you go.'

'Drew?' Alison said softly to the very still figure lying in the hospital bed.

11

Somehow she'd thought that he would have wires and tubes all over his body which would make hugging him difficult and was relieved to find that he didn't, that all he had was an intravenous drip in his arm.

Of course he had a big bandage around his head and a bulky cast on his leg under the covers, but she'd expected those things. She'd also expected that he'd be woozy and probably not say much because the intern had warned her that his thoughts would be muddled.

He had told her to hold Drew's hand instead. He'd told her that twice, as if in her emotional state she'd become stupid as well.

'Drew?' she said again softly.

But Drew didn't open his eyes. His hands were lying on top of the covers, and Alison obediently took the hand nearest her, and like Robbie before her held it between her own.

Drew's hand was cold, but not freezing, but it was bunched up into a fist. Alison, knowing what it meant when hands were balled into fists, caressed the knuckles and then turned his hand over and gently began to draw back the fingers.

It didn't take her long because Drew's usual strength and virility seemed to be all but sapped. She watched his face intently as she eased open his fingers, hoping he would open his eyes.

He didn't have to say anything. She only needed eye contact to tell him how much she loved him and that she forgave him for everything if there was, in fact, anything to forgive.

Staring at his face now with a palpable longing that ached all though her body, she drew back the last little finger and placed his open palm absentmindedly alongside him on the covers.

Then, overcome by emotion, she leaned over to kiss him, and, as she did so, she saw something astonishingly beautiful resting on his palm, something cupped in his hand like an offering.

Her engagement ring.

'Oh, Drew,' she said in a huge, quavering gasp.

Quickly she picked the ring up off his palm, and slid it back on to her waiting, trembling finger. Then she did what she'd been about to do before, she leaned over and kissed him.

He opened his eyes, focused.

'Ali?' he said.

'Drew — '

Drew tried to make his mouth work to say something else, but all he could manage was 'Robbie'.

'Robbie's fine,' she told him.

Drew tried again, speaking slowly.

'Will you ever forgive me?'

'Shush,' she said, talking over the top of him. 'There's nothing to forgive.'

He said thickly. 'I love you, Alison Whitehead.'

'I love you, too,' she said gently, her eyes filling with tears.

He reached for her hand.

'Don't let me go to sleep again,' he said, but his eyes were closing. 'I have so much to tell you . . . about Robbie. Robbie,' he repeated, almost with reverence.

Alison nodded.

She looked at Drew with shining eyes, but he seemed to have drifted off again.

'I have something to tell you, too,' she said to no-one in particular, 'but it can wait until tomorrow.'

'What?' Drew said sleepily. 'What . . . do you have to tell me?'

'Oh,' Alison said. 'You're not asleep.'

He shook his head imperceptibly.

'I just can't . . . can't keep my eyes open,' he told her.

He waited, but she said nothing.

'What?' he said again. 'What is it?'

'It's something I want,' she said, suddenly nervous. 'I mean, something I'd like . . . but of course I don't have to have it.' What if he didn't want what she wanted?

'You know I'd try to give you anything you wanted,' Drew told her.

'I know,' she said. 'I know you would.'

Drew forced his eyes open.

Alison looked at him.

'I want a baby,' she said softly. 'Your baby.'

Drew couldn't speak, he tried to but he was overwhelmed, but he realised he had to say something, even if it was with his eyes.

But he had to squint though because the light in the room suddenly seemed so awfully bright.

It seemed to him that the elusive sliver of shimmering moonlit sea that he'd seen so recently from his loft and taken to be a sign of happiness beyond his reach, was wafting all around him and Alison, bathing them both in a soft and warm glow.

Drew smiled at Alison, a silly, dopey smile because his mouth muscles still weren't working properly.

And Alison, seeing his smile, smiled too, and leaned over and kissed him again.

THE END

We do hope that you have enjoyed reading this large print book.

Did you know that all of our titles are available for purchase?

We publish a wide range of high quality large print books including:
Romances, Mysteries, Classics
General Fiction
Non Fiction and Westerns

Special interest titles available in large print are:
The Little Oxford Dictionary
Music Book, Song Book
Hymn Book, Service Book

Also available from us courtesy of Oxford University Press:
Young Readers' Dictionary
(large print edition)
Young Readers' Thesaurus
(large print edition)

For further information or a free brochure, please contact us at:
Ulverscroft Large Print Books Ltd.,
The Green, Bradgate Road, Anstey,
Leicester, LE7 7FU, England.
Tel: (00 44) **0116 236 4325**
Fax: (00 44) **0116 234 0205**

DON'T TOUCH ME

John Russell Fearn

A jewel heist goes wrong when the escaping robbers abduct Gloria Vane, the beautiful film actress. Then as gang leader Ace Monohan falls for Gloria, it leads to dissension amongst his men, and the destruction and abandonment of his hideout. Ace, forced to go on the run, takes the stolen jewels with him. Now Gloria finds herself at the mercy of rival gangster 'Fingers' Baxter, who plans to use her to lure Ace out of hiding . . .

THE LEGACY OF THE TOWER

Sheila Lewis

Lizanne Naismith is saddened when Jeffrey Falkin, owner of her former ancestral home, Gilliestoun Tower, dies in an accident. The grief of his family turns to shock and denial when an unknown son, Alex, turns up. Lizanne is the only one to befriend him, much to the chagrin of her boyfriend Steven, Jeffrey's son. Using her skills as a researcher she investigates Alex's mysterious background. When a long-buried secret is revealed, it alters the lives of everyone involved.

A TIME TO DANCE

Eileen Stafford

Deborah thinks that nothing exciting happens in wartime Bristol. But then the Americans arrive, preparing to fight in occupied Europe. And for Deborah, everything changes. She finds excitement when she meets Warren and falls in love. But her romantic dreams are shattered when her father sends her away to live with her aunt in Exmouth. And more heartbreak follows when she feels forced to seek refuge in London. At the end of the war — can she ever find happiness again?

HIS LITTLE GIRL

Liz Fielding

Staying alone at her brother-in-law's cottage on a stormy night, Dora finds an intruder in the house, a man called John Gannon. He's clearly a man on the run, but Dora is charmed by him — and the adorable little girl in his arms. She decides to help Gannon, a devoted father, willing to do anything to keep Sophie safe. Too bad the only thing keeping Dora safe from Gannon is his misconception that she is Richard's wife . . .

LEGACY OF LOVE

Dorothy Taylor

Bookseller Kay Deacon learns that she has been left part of the late Tobias Garner's collection of antique books on condition she brings his records up to date. So when Tobias's nephew Marshall Garner accuses her of cultivating the old man's affections, Kay resolves to carry out Tobias's wishes and prove that she is not a gold digger. But when she begins to find herself entangled in a web of deceit, her own life is in danger . . .

THE VALIANT FOOL

Valerie Holmes

Emma Frinton, a captain's daughter, is forced to live in reduced circumstances in a humble cottage in the small fishing village of Ebton, when the French imprison her father. Emma and her mother, Lydia, accept leaving their beloved home in Whitby, but neither of them anticipates the consequences of Emma's kindly actions when she stumbles across an injured man on the dunes. In saving Montgomery Wild's life, she unwittingly finds the key to unlock their family's future.